ABOUT BEING LOVED ...

ABOUT BEING LOVED ...
A Passion Worth Fighting For

Michael Ware Hollingsworth

MAGNIF
publishing

ABOUT BEING LOVED ... A Passion Worth Fighting For
Copyright © 2023 Michael Ware Hollingsworth

Magnif Publishing, West Hollywood CA. All rights reserved. Printed in The United States of America. No part of this book may be used or reproduced in any matter whatsoever without written permission from the author except in the case of brief quotations embodied in critical articles and reviews. This is a work of fiction. Names and characters are the product of the author's imagination. Any resemblance to actual persons is entirely coincidental.

To contact the author: Lmagnif@sbcglobal.net or 323.650.8223

ISBN 9798853644892

This collection of free verse prose is dedicated is to the
following fabulous men who have in some way touched
my life through their love, their kindness, their being,
their help, their bodies, their minds, and their spirit…

Thank you Michael, Gordon, Bob, Peter, Larry, Jerry,
Fred, Ron, Charles, Jeff, Gary, Jim, Lou, and Tommy…

And a special dedication to my friend Mark Franklin,
whose brief life brought joy to so many people…
Thank you, Mark for teaching me so much
about the music you brought to my life,
and the world; I miss you.

Author's Note

Some years ago when the wheels fell off, I realized it was time to get sober, which is what I did, and then realized it was time to go home back to Los Angeles, which is what I did. You see, there were no palm trees in Central Park.

Now the reason for this book of free form prose and poetry was cathartic. Of course, I met someone, who proceeded to break my heart. Not that I'm the first to have my heart broken—but when you're newly sober, the pain is a little interesting. No, not interesting; it gets more than your interest. It grabs your full attention and also, it hurts like a son-of-a-bitch. So, I asked myself, how do I heal and get through this pain and still remain on the planet? Well, I got out my thumb drive, plugged it in to that little slot and wrote this little book you're about to read.

By the way, I didn't use real names, so that the guilty party who almost killed my heart, wouldn't get the satisfaction of knowing they could inspire these words. If you're sensing bitterness or resentment within me—no, not now; yes once, but not now. So, I give you, *About Being Loved…*

Vignettes

About Being Loved	1
About Being Gay	5
Snowy Days	10
In My Sight	13
Afterwork	16
One of Those Days	19
Taking A Risk	25
The Morning After The Night Before	28
No	31
The Moment I Knew	33
Saying It	37
In Love Again	41
Making Love In Love	42
Watching You Sleep	46
How Do You Describe Love?	48
Putting Me On The Spot	50
The Ceremony	52
Larry to Drew	54
A Day In The Life	59
Nothing's Perfect	69
Little Ol' Me	75
Our First Fight	90
If	99
Sunday In The Park with Drew and Larry	101
Billy Rutger	103
Yes…We're Guilty	118
Just Below The Surface	124

Once The Passion Goes	128
The Night Before Leaving For The Coast	130
Spanish Tiles and Palm Trees	132
And Now, A Word From The West Coast	135
That Day	139
Many Things Will Change	144
River, Hell…I Damn Near Cried An Ocean	147
Is It Door Number…	154
Comparing Him To You	158
Subtext-Aftermath-Drew	163
Subtext-Aftermath-Larry	167
A Conversation Overheard	169
Dazed On The Throne	175
Answering Machine Chronicles	177
Something You'll Never Know	185
Over The Rainbow	187
The Importance	190
Epilogue	194
Acknowledgments	209

About Being Loved...

About Being loved...
Isn't that what life's about?
About being loved or trying to be loved,
It's about buying,
The right cologne,
The right toothpaste,
The right blue jeans...
You know the ones I mean,
The ones that make your ass look tight...
Your basket look bigger...
That's what we buy into.
Whatever we can do for ourselves
To be the best we can be
To look the best we can look
So that someone might
Just like what they see and love us...L-O-V-E us...
That's really all we want.

Being loved is only important
If you're not.
That's when you feel less than...
When you don't feel loved...
Myself included,
I must admit

Some of us
Desperately want to be loved

But we don't know how to go about it…
How to approach the subject
With another human being we want to love us.
You can't just ask someone
To fall in love with you on the spot…
If we could…
Wouldn't that make it easy?
Adios blue jeans and toothpaste business…
Wouldn't we be fabulous without all those trappings?

The truth is,
Most of us are a little afraid,
Especially here on the semi-semi
Tropical island of Concreta,
Also known as Manhattan,
We've all bought into the idea
That we don't have time to find love,
Or need to be loved for that matter,
Because we're too busy with,
Careers, investments
Finding ourselves (that's so West Coast)
But spreading fast to the East
A new book,
Anything, any excuse,
Any alibi, even exercise,
To deal with the issue of LOVE!
About being loved…
I'm in total agreement
It's rough thinking of myself being in love

Giving my power away,
Let alone my heart.

I'm afraid,
That's the real truth.
I think about being loved and in love,
At least every waking minute
And I don't remember all my dreams
So I may think about it when I'm
Sleeping
Shaving
Showering
Getting my shoes shined.

I always feel a little tinge of disappointment
When I see a couple…
Any kind of couple…
Holding hands
Or stealing those special little glances.

I use the thoughts about being loved
Anywhere I'm uncomfortable.
Those thoughts get me through
The night and the day…
After having been in love
And having been loved
I sometimes think it will never happen again
But I do surrender to whatever does happen,
Which is what I have done now.
My attitude is fuck it!

I'm here and plan to remain here,
And live my life to the fullest
Whatever that is…
So, if I fall in love,
Fabulous…
If not,
Not so fabulous…
About being loved…
That's what I have to say about being loved,
And I hope that one day,
I am again!

About Being Gay

Yesiree, ladies and gentlemen,
I am gay,
A homosexual...
Or any of those other disgusting slurs you might use
Like queer, fag, pansy, poofter, fairy...
But at the same time,
I am a policeman,
A doctor,
A lawyer,
A priest,
A brilliantly gifted actor...
A singer,
A judge,
A writer,
But most of all,
I am a human being.

If I don't receive nurturing,
Or love,
Or Spiritual guidance,
Pieces of me die,
Until there's nothing left...

I do want your son,
If he's over 21,
Sexy, intelligent, handsome, and gay...
Otherwise mothers,
Your son is safe...

There are misconceptions about gays
And homosexuality,
The difference being between gays and straight
Is three drinks and a Molly…Just kidding!
The difference is only in the bedroom…
And I'll admit we have to improvise a bit.
But we experience wonderful sex lives.

When two men fall in love
They share the same incredible feelings
That straight people do…
That "right" person comes along,
With all the feelings attached…
Bells ring
There is a weakness in the knees and stomach
You become light-headed
And suddenly…the world is right.

I used to hate being gay,
Because of ignorance and the stigma
But now I'm happy and grateful
I am who I am.
My life is wonderful
Though not always fulfilled,
Except, when I'm in love…
There's that word again…
There are magic connotations
Anytime that word is used,
Well Hell, love is magic!

Being a happy gay man,
I consider myself an expert on the subject...
So, let's straighten out one misconception now...
You do not suddenly become gay...
You are born that way...
Yes, sorry Jerry Falwell, Brigham Young, and Pat Robertson.
That once you are gay...
You do not become straight, unless you're faking it...
No matter how hard you try...
You can live a straight life
And bullshit yourself and half the world,
But you will always know!
You are who you are.

Being gay feels like being straight...
You exist and live...
You can participate in your life
Or you can say poor me
And wallow in the lot you have been given,
Being gay means you are a little more considerate,
You have a lot of passion for many things
And you're the first to be there for a cause
Any cause that promotes life and the arts...
Sometimes you try too hard to be funny
Sometimes we're too bitchy and sarcastic...
And bitter...
We become afraid...
Afraid we will grow old
Without ever having been loved or having loved.
We buy into that bullshit also...

And start believing it,
And it manifests itself,
And then many of us end up on barstools
At the neighborhood wrinkle room.

Once again, it's all about being loved…
And we really know how to love
Once the opportunity arises…
And in love we will give
Until there is nothing left to give…
Ever been to a gay guy's house at Christmas
When he is in love?
If you have
You know where the term fairyland came from.

Most of us have been so damn angry,
At one time or another,
Because of discrimination
Or from being called names
Or maybe because we try too hard
To be happy that it becomes phony.
And yes…
There is a great underlying sadness
But most gay men I know are trying to recover…
As long as we know
That it will take some time,
We'll be okay being gay.

I should probably have mentioned
It…

You know, the thing...
The disease...
Well, I am guilty
Of putting my head in the sand like
An ostrich...
But this is a love story...
And it is mentioned later.

One more thought...though a little bitchy,
Ask Butch the truck driver,
How many chapel ceilings he's painted?

Snowy Days

There's nothing sadder
Than the grayness of Manhattan
On a snowy day
As you see it from the floor to ceiling windows
Of your oh-so-drop-dead
Decorated-to-death Upper Westside apartment
With the view of Central Park and the Hudson
And you have nothing to do
And you are
Alone…
And it's a snowy day
And yes damnit,
Here you are,
The King of the castle
Without a loyal subject
Or a consort
Or a peasant
Or a willing phone number
To share your wishes, demands, or needs with
And Hell yes it hurts,

Well screw it!
I don't want to leave my space
For the space of some uppity museum
Or to go skating in Wollman Rink.
Those things are best enjoyed
With one other,

Especially on a snowy day with one other
Be the other significant or not.
When you share a snowy day with someone,
You may have to listen to
Idle chatter,
You may have to laugh,
And break your concentration,
You might have to touch someone,
Or they might touch you...
Ah ha, and then you just might have to admit it...
You like it...
You'll probably break down
And also admit that you...
Yeah, you...
Old stalwart, stout-hearted you
Needs to be out there
Spilling your guts,
Ripping open your heart,
Just to see what happens
And God forbid
Someone might grab
That silly old heart
And take it away
And play with it,
Or perhaps cherish it for a milli-second
Or maybe even hand it back to you
Looking like a piece of hamburger
As you see the shape
Of their beautiful ass
Going through the door

For the last time
With nothing more
Than a careless wave for all your trouble,
And…you…are…paralyzed…with…
PAIN…
That could kill an army
Dead in its tracks
And that's the way you feel,
Dead as a stone…
Your emptiness could fill a basin
And each fiber of your being
Is screaming to escape
From the loneliness…
Because there is this need
Deep within you
To be held and touched and loved…
Especially on a snowy day…
Especially on this Goddamn snow day…

In My Sight

Thank you, Bushnell...
Thank you for making those fabulous binoculars.
And thank you Mr. James C. Burton
For leaving them in the cab.
Oh, and by all means,
Thank you, Mr. and Mrs. Whoever you are
For producing the object of my affection
On the other end of these binoculars.

Yes, you there in the park.
I don't know your name,
Or your age,
Or your dislikes,
Or your weight,
Though I would say 170 pounds.

I know your taste in clothes
And I concur.
You look great in gray.
Forget the tie with the aqua accents.
Wear the one with the petite stripes of
Magenta and cerise with that suit.

You love that dog, don't you?
No ring on your finger...no Mrs.?
No more cigarettes?
It must be twelve days for you.

I've been watching you for three weeks.
I'm proud of you,
Smoking's tough to quit.
It's been one year and three months for me.
Coffee is next…no it's not.

The clock says 7:43 A.M.,
You're very punctual.
I wonder if you jog?
I'm not early enough to catch you at that.
I also wonder what you do for a living…
Pin stripe…Wall Street no doubt.

I wish I were not so damn shy,
Or I would come down and just ask you.
You may think I'm forward,
You might not even be a "member" of my club,
Although I think you are.

It's been a while since I've been in love,
I've been buried in my work…
My desk is at the window…
When I can't write I cruise the park
With some binoculars I found in a cab.

Don't leave me yet…
I guess it's time for work…
I forget how lucky I am to be able to
Set my own hours.
Goodbye for now!

You don't know me yet,
But you will,
I have to make the right move,
Move carefully,
Size you up,
You may not even be interested,
But then maybe…yes.

I've watched you enough
To know your tastes in people.
I fit in…
Or should I say,
I want to fit in…
I want to taste your lips!

Afterwork

Thank God you're finally there…
Maybe I can get some work done now…
I fucking hate obsessions
I need my mind to be free
I must think with my head
And feel with my body
Not feel with my head
And think with my body…
I am a chicken shit…
I should have come downstairs
Leave the safety of my apartment
Come into the park
Ask you about your dog
See if you have a case of acne
Or bad breath
Any reason please God
To stop thinking I want you…

I am a writer for God sakes!
I need to concentrate
It's tough enough to face this white bull.
I am beginning to act like a crazy person,
That's dangerous…
They will not put you away for being crazy,
Only acting as if.
Five weeks now I have been watching you
I know your routines…

I don't need this in my life...
Yes I do...
No, I really don't
I am plain and simple
I need only facts
Not fantasies or obsessions.
I need reality
I see you
I did not imagine you...
Please stay there...
Don't move...
I'm coming down to the park
I'm getting rid of you...
Once and for all!
I will be so obnoxious
You will say fuck off
Before I even get a chance to know you
That will fix me...I mean it!

Come on elevator
Two grand a month rent
And two hours for the elevator
I'm gonna move...I swear...
No, I'm not...
I love the view...
Just what the Hell am I doing!
I am thirty-four,
Acting like I'm fourteen,
But he is gorgeous
This is absurd...come on feet

Back to the apartment,
Back to the window…
Pick up the binoculars…
Damn…
He's gone…

One of Those Days

I hate this kind of day…
One of those Saturdays…
One of those shit New York
I don't have anything to do today
Except get dressed
Looking as good as I can
And then I'll hit the gourmet section
On the sixth floor
Of…with nothing better to do than go
To Bloomingdale's kind of days.
What to wear?
Not the jeans
Even if they are acid washed Guess.
Maybe the Laredo pants
Won't see many of those
Since they came from L.A.
Yeah…and they make the old tush look tight
Let's see…the suede dingo boots
The turquoise Navaho shirt,
And oh yes, the bolo tie.
Not bad for thirty-four.

Nice day…
Through the park today
I can stop by that new Cajun place
The one on East 60th…
Just to check the menu…

Or maybe to the museum…
No…Bloomingdales…
Also, I want to see how the rich folks live.
One day I'll have a townhouse here
If I'm not too damn old to enjoy it…
No, I won't…I love the west side.

Bloomies isn't so bad…
Once you get through the first floor.
It always reminds me of a disco…
All that gold and black
And instant anxiety,
Until I get to the housewares department
And decompress in a little peace and quiet.

I have sneaking suspicion about New Yorkers
And the kitchen department of Bloomingdale's
That once you buy that unique kitchen gadget,
And we've all bought them,
When you put it in the drawer,
It stays there.
I have every gadget Bloomie's has ever sold
Which makes sense as over the last three years
I've had three dinner parties for 12
But as more Yuppies are produced
And food continues as a Yuppie hobby,
So shall the gourmet department of Bloomie's thrive.

Over to the gourmet coffee section…
What is this my poor old eyes

Are beholding without benefit of Bushnells...
It's him...
Yes, it is...
But I'm not in the mood to cruise
I came here to shop...
Where's the exit...
Just a glance...
Oh my God,
I don't believe your eyes...
I have never seen such a shade of green
Jesus, where have you been all my life?
Well maybe in late spring you see green like that
Am I being obvious?
Holy shit...you're the guy from the park
The love of my life
The man of my dreams...
Right here in Bloomies
Is this a mistake
Is it Divine Order?
Are you looking at me...
I think you are.
I will definitely avoid your eyes,
The most beautiful baleful green eyes
I have ever stared into...
That are staring into...
Yes, you are, aren't you...
Now what?

Yes, I am shy,
I'll just see if you really are interested

Over to potholders…
The best selection in the world
Yuk! How about these chartreuse ones?
That buyer was fired…
Never chartreuse in a princess's kitchen,
And a queen…well, please!
My, isn't this Spanish platter shiny?
In fact, I can see your reflection over my shoulder
You are watching

Oh, a food processor demonstration,
Let's see,
Thirty things to do with a zucchini…
I can think of one more…
But you don't need a food processor for it.

You're following me…
Now what do I do?
I'm not ready for this today.

Should I start a conversation
If I do,
Will he hear my knees shaking?
Is that his hand he's sticking out?
And he's saying my name is Larry Barton…
Nice to meet you…my name is Drew Saban

You followed me here…
You've seen me watching you in the park
When you happen to look up at my building

And wondered why I never came over
To say hello?
You saw me today and followed me here?
Yes, I'd love to have lunch…yes
I don't care which restaurant…
Have I been to Jack's?
The restaurant with those wonderful double height windows
That overlook East 73rd Street?
Yes, I'd love to.

I don't believe I'm so quiet,
Letting you do all the talking…
You are so easy to be with…
Yes, I would like to go to the theater
You have an extra ticket to…
No, I haven't seen *Sunday In the Park With George*, I lied
I can damn near recite every word
And lyric by heart.
"Finishing the Hat" is my favorite
Sondheim song of all time…
You'll pick me up!
You have a car and driver…
I'm impressed
Yes, I would like to walk back
Through the park with you…
You're kidding,
You're renting on the Westside
Two blocks from where I live.
You've bought an apartment on Park
And it's being redone…

                Yes, I love winter in New York
                Oh, you were watching the dog for a friend.
SUBTEXT (I would love to any day, anywhere with this man)
                It seemed like the ordinary 30-minute walk
                Was over in five minutes.
                I feel as if I could float to my apartment
                Without using the elevator
                God knows I would get there faster.
                Thank you, Mr. Bloomingdale,
                For changing my life forever!

Taking A Risk

Eventually you get to the point
Where you have to throw all caution
To the wind no matter what direction
And put your old ass on the line
Without a friggin' thought
To the consequences of the moment or second
Or for the year for that matter.
You just let that old heart wander out there
That heart that's been closed
As tight as a bass drum
With a lock that is rusted shut
And here comes this person with a crowbar
And perfect direction in his eyes
That nothing will deter,
And like a dagger
He is heading straight for your heart
And he gets inside you
Wedges himself right in there
And you resist like the same ends of a magnet
And really get pissed off,
Because he found a way into Fort Heart!
(Had your strategy down…huh, Ace?)
Then all those little soldiers
You had around you for defense
Like…
Not enough time to date,

And sarcasm,
And brilliant bitter quips,
The kind that cut right to the bone
Fall to the wayside
As you stand there helpless
As a feather in the wind
While Prince Charming comes along
And is willing to see through all
The bullshit from Prince Precious
And maybe he takes a little patience
And understanding to find out
Just why your heart is so hidden
And then you have to notice
Hey! This one isn't running off
Like the others did.
Why is he hanging around?
He wants to take you out again…
Like he said he had a ball on the first date…
Likes your sense of humor
Your clothes…
The restaurant you picked…Vanessa's in the Village
Carmen McRae at the Blue Note
Late supper at the Algonquin…
You did everything right…
And yet…They're the things you like to do,
And he likes you for it…
And you really like him…
More than you've liked anyone
In a long time.

And you miss him already,
And he's only been gone ten minutes
And then he calls you the next day
To confirm your date and you're elated
And you decide to take a risk
And say...
Yes!

The Morning After the Night Before

Just now watching you leave,
I am relieved…but a little sad.
I didn't think this was going to happen
But God knows
I hoped it would…
I manipulated you
And used every trick in the book.

And it was Goddamn wonderful…
And you were wonderful
And I am ecstatic to think
I will see you tonight.

I have known since the moment
I met you at Bloomingdale's…
Sort of like putting a transmission into gear…
You are the one
There is no doubt about it…
The one I've waited for all my life.

All the anticipation…
Wondering what it would be like
When all along I knew…just knew
It would be right because it was with you
And because my emotions were coming
Straight from my heart

As were yours
And the time passed so quickly
And we didn't want to stop
And we didn't give a damn
If we were both exhausted
And bone tired
And completely spent...

This is life at its best
This is me giving without reservation
And me taking without guilt
And you giving your all
And taking my all
And I am willing to give it all
Again, and again and again
And isn't it right?
I feel like I've known you thirty years
Not thirty days.
I am slipping though,
I can't believe we waited...
Waited until the third date...
Although I could hardly wait
But it was wonderful getting to know you
Outside of the bed
And what a departure that has been for me...
But there would have been hell to pay
If you had made me wait much longer
And there lies the difference
It is different
I am different since you touched me

I hope you're different since I touched you
I can translate all of this into breath
All the time waiting for you to arrive
My breath was tight
It came in little gasps…
My mind was saying
Will he like me
Is this just a pastime with him?
Does he date others too?
Will he hate the restaurant?
Will he be bored
And what if we get into bed
And my body turns him off
I don't go to the gym
Or I don't do the things in bed
You know…the things he likes
Or maybe he doesn't do what I like…
Can't worry about it now…
Because thank you God
For the perfect night
With the perfect man
The perfect plan
For making me aware I may have
To face the possibility again
That maybe I could entertain the fact
That maybe…just maybe
I could love this man!

No

No is an important word
One of the most
If not the most important word
Not in the context of let's say…
No, I'm hungry
    Or
No, not that movie
    Or
No, I don't want to leave
    Or
No, I'm not having an affair, are you?
And of course, the worst is
No, he says he doesn't love me anymore
That one's absolutely annihilating,
Especially when you are making
Exceptional deals with God
In hopes that you will hear from him…
No, I'm not having an affair
God yes, I still love you…

So then you don't have to say…
No, I'm not crying
There's something in my eye
What's worse than no
Is the uncertainty
That accompanies another important word
A word

That quite simply is capable

Of driving you crazy…

The word is maybe!

Maybe we should see a musical tonight

Maybe the ballet

Anything in a theater

Maybe a movie

Maybe we should hit Tino's

And meet my friend Tommy Corcoran for dinner

For great pasta and warmth

Besides, Barney the waiter

Is the best in New York

    Or

Maybe we should put a log on the fire

    And

Chill down some champagne

    And

Put some Rupert Holmes on the stereo

      And light some candles

    And

Then consume each other's body

    Or

Why don't we take no and maybe,

And make them a definite yes….

The Moment I Knew

You have been trite,

The surprise,

And you have been the unexpected.

You have brought such incredible

Excitement to my life

That I am spoiled for all ages.

The word is texture…

No…not texture.

Sheen,

Maybe that is a good word to use

And I never know what to expect.

Although extravagant…

The night you chartered the yacht "Entrepreneur"

For a cruise around Manhattan.

Just the two of us…

A band for dancing…

An incredible dinner served

By waiters in white gloves…

That is hard to top!

And then the flight aboard

A private jet to Atlantic City,

What a surprise that was…

Just because I said I love Dianna Ross.

I'm creative,
But I would never have thought of that.

As we went on all these excursions,
I knew you were a special man,
And the stirrings were there,
And I tried to keep the lid on them,
I just didn't want to rush things.
And then for my birthday,
It would take someone like you,
To know that there is a closed subway station
At 57th & 8th.

I don't know how you pulled it off
Getting through all the red tape
In this Berg, but you did it
And I was so impressed.
Tonight, you topped yourself.
I should have guessed something was up
When you said not to dress,
As we dress for dinner most nights.

So, you arrive you crazy person
Very casual with a picnic hamper.

Now I know it's too cold to be outside.
You tell me to leave the bedroom
For a while… And when I come back
I don't believe it!
You nut. You wonderful nut.

You have brought fake grass
And laid it on top of my bed.
There are candles everywhere...

Every detail...
Right down to the seashells
For the salt and pepper.
It was so sweet I wanted to cry
And almost did.

And the food...
Pecan chicken from Word of Mouth!
Along with new potato salad,
From Zabar's, and an incredible Brie.
Cornbread and ribs from Carolina's.
And to start, a bottle of Cristal '79.
The Joseph Drouihan Puligny Montrachet.
And the best ever chocolate mousse.

You kept asking me why I'm
So quiet since I usually chatter
A mile a minute.
It's because I'm touched.
Not only at the expense of this meal,
But I know all the trouble you went to
To bring it here.

No one has ever done the things for me
You have.
No one has ever been as thoughtful

And caring.
No one has ever made me feel so
Loved…with sheen and polish
In my life.

As I savored every morsel,
And you held me in your arms
When we were finished,
I just reflected on how far we've come
On this little trip down lover's lane.
I watched the flames dancing on the log,
And I'm sure I saw the flames
Spell out I Love You…
That's when I knew.
That's the moment I knew,
I…Love…You!

Saying It

After being able to take only so much
…Of fighting it
…Then seeing it clearly
I am losing the battle
Although I worked so damn hard to resist…
Right to the frigging brink
Where I don't even own my feelings any longer,
This isn't pain
But a constant state of confusion
Disorientation, silliness, permanent arousal…
I can no more describe
What I am feeling
Than I can write a Beethoven movement
From memory.
I am happy
And scared
And wary…
Intimidated…
But most of all
Cautious and afraid
To completely throw myself out there.

What is new is this state of Euphoria
In finding that with each day
My feelings grow
And I look forward to your visit
So I can feel your skin

Right next to mine
As I kiss the nape of your neck
Pass my fingers through your hair
Feel you slip your arms around me
And know that when that contact is made
I lose my breath
My stomach gets queasy
My legs are weak
There's a cold sweat
I'm in constant submission
I can't wait to get you out of your clothes,
Most of my pants and shirts are missing a button
And then what a sight to behold…
You there with those green eyes
And when I see them
Well, the rest of the world
Just simply does not exist

Don't get me wrong…
I have built a wonderful defense against it…
A mechanism to protect myself
Myself and my heart that is
From all I just said…
No sir
I will protect myself from strange feelings
Within my body…

I have to be very careful to be careful
And take little steps
As I become aware of how

Just how you were feeling towards me
And when we made love
I knew it
Felt it
Tried to reject it
Then couldn't and wouldn't
And now
I'm in one Hell of a mess
There's nowhere to run
I've been consumed, contained, and controlled…
I hate it at the same time I want it
But I will not
I repeat
Will not…cannot
No matter what
Will not say it
Not even in passion will I
Let those words escape…
Not fall from these lips
Sealed like Tut's tomb…

Wait a damn minute…
Wait…
Last night…
No it couldn't be…
Was it you…

Couldn't have been me…
But damn it, someone said it
Ah shit, yes damn it

I did it

I said it

And I swore to God I would never ever

Be the first to say it…

Never again…

But I did…

I said those fucking words…

Those terrible awful words that rule the world…

I…Love…You!

In Love Again

There goes my heart,
In love again,
Sailed off my sleeve straight to you,
Still on the mend,
In love again, In love again,

Hearts not too strong,
Still black and blue,
Over the pain of that love,
Now it's too soon,
To be with you, in love again,

My foolish heart,
Won't listen to me,
I tell it that love is too hot,
And if careful it's not,
It will burn,
Won't ever learn,
This heart of mine,

Is that my heart,
Beating so strong,
Filled up with passion once more,
And a new song,
Singing to me,
You're in love again,
In love again.

Making Love in Love

The difference is how I feel,

How I respond,

How you respond,

How you feel

The way your eyes take on that dreamy look

The way your hands gently wash over me

In one long caress instead of merely touching.

No matter how tight we hold each other,

It's never close enough

It's as if we try to become one through osmosis

Those little flicks of your lips on my skin

Gentle as the rustle of a maiden's crinolines

Billowed by a spring breeze.

What a beautiful sight…

Me watching the crown of your head

As you take that slow breathy journey

Descending the contours of my chest

Bare as a prairie…

Then you nibble my pelvic bones

Faintly sucking them with your lips…

I simply go away…

To where, I don't know

That's the opening chapter

Your skillful lips know just how

To surprise the soft flesh of my inner thighs

As I barely keep from fainting

While your tongue bathes my legs
All The way down to my ankles

By now I'm covered with a vague cold sweat
As fine as a morning mist
I tangle my fingers in your chestnut hair
Watching the top of your dappled shoulders
Still a pale gold from that Bermuda weekend...
Then you move back up and I
Thrash and moan as you...oh yes...there,
Right there
Find the magic spot on my neck...
Yes...yes kiss me there
Please stop, don't...
How did you learn to kiss like that?

Make it last
And just as I think I want you...
You wait...
I almost lose my mind...
Oh God...please hold me...
And then you take me in your warm mouth
So slow...then faster...faster...
Oh Christ...it's building...
The hot liquid of life about to erupt
From my body...
And just as it is about to find freedom
You stop...I gasp
I want you and you know it...
Can you hear my heart screaming for you?

Every nerve in my body responds in tandem
Why am I out of breath?
Now as we're just starting to consume each other
The stubble of your beard brushes the tip of my penis
So stiff it might break…
As we reverse and I take you…
I feel your heartbeat…your pulse
You're mine, I'm yours
Let me be the one to touch you
In a way that no one's ever touched you before
And you'll know you're loved!

Yes, I submit to you
Submit as you pin my arms to my sides
Okay…alright
Do what you will…
Whatever you want
I want you
In the worst way…please
I want you now…
Make love to me…please
Make love to me as only you can…
God in heaven…yes
That's it…Make me feel loved now…
So good…I'm about to lose consciousness
And that incredible music…
Steve Reich and 58 voices

Oh Christ it gets better each time
And I didn't think it could
Now please

That's the way I want to feel
Touch me there so gently
Yes I feel it
I know
It's the best
Yes I want more
Just know this body is here for you
I was born to be with you
I know you're in me
I'm in you
I can't even tell where you end, and I begin
I only know I've loved you forever...
In the plan of the universe
This was a page
Meant to happen
Making love with the one
You love
When you're in love!

Watching You Sleep

I think I'm so clever…
I wake up early…before you do
That's so I can run a brush through my hair
Do my meditation…
That's so I can touch base with reality…
I still don't believe you're mine
That this incredible human specimen…
The one in my bed is you.
I try to look my best when you wake up
But I ain't ever gonna look like you…
So, I stopped trying. Not that I'm that bad

I love to watch you sleep
I love the peace on your face
The gentle heaving of your chest
With that half smile on your face
And I always wonder what you dream about.
Have you gone to someplace I know nothing of?
Are you thinking of me?
Or maybe you're thinking of that stock deal
Which will pay for the mortgage on the house
On Fire Island for just the two of us…
Or maybe you're not
I hope so…
You there sleeping…
I cannot even tell you how much I love you
And how you've enriched my life

My world
My being
It's as if all has become simplicity
I have the universe figured out…
There's you…
There's me…
And all we need is time…
Time to consume each other.
Since you've been part of my life
The only time I own is when I sleep…
The rest belongs to you…

I love to watch your back
To see the smooth skin
(Except for that mole)
I would caress you
But I know you need to sleep
Especially after last night
Especially after last night
Isn't that what we're here for?
To love each other to the limit…
And then sleep to refresh?

How Do You Describe Love?

How do you describe love?

I'm not sure

But I'm willing to try…

Let's see…

A partnership between two people

Who absolutely

Adore

And

Cherish

And

Treasure

And

Forgive

And Delight

And Find pleasure

In knowing

The other's mere presence is enough

To want to make a commitment

To the other

In hopes that it will last forever.

Love is simply

Holding a trusted hand

As you take a weekend jaunt

By a picturesque stream

And because your heart has been opened

You notice the froth in the stream

As it courses over moss-covered pebbles.

Love is a feeling of the other's presence
And not having to say a word…
It's a Saturday afternoon
When you've been shopping
And there's a ritual of going out on a Saturday night
But what you're both feeling
Is let's send out for Chinese
Light a fire
Watch the tube and then…
And you both know at the same time
As you tell the cab driver to turn around
And take you back home…
And at the same time, you both remember
To call the restaurant and cancel the reservation.

It's the way you find yourself
With a half-smile on your face most of the time…
That your friends describe as silly
And his good points far outweigh the bad…
You know you're safe with him…
You'll always be safe with the one you love…
That's how I describe love…

Just one more thing…
Gazing into eyes…
To get a reading on the world.

Putting Me On The Spot

I get a little pissed at you
When you put me on the spot
And you ask me
Why do you love me?
You don't have to ask that…
I just love…
Can you tell me exactly why you love me?
No, you can't…
Give me an uninterrupted month
And it's possible I can tell you…
But what the Hell…
It doesn't matter…
The important thing is
You love me…
I love you…
That is…
For the time being…
For today.
Actually,
I never tell you
How much I love you
And why I love you
You're warm
And
Tender
And Gentle
And Funny and

Honest

And your jokes are worse than Carson's

But I laugh...

'Cause they're your jokes.

But it's the way you make me feel,

And the WAY you make me feel...

That is so important

Yeah, that's it

I feel important

Because I feel loved...

What more could I want?

The Ceremony

I could break the fourth wall and tell you
We were ahead of our time
You'll see why
The ultimate test for this love affair
Came when I introduced Larry
To my best friend Billy Rutger.
We went to his terrace overlooking
The Hudson for drinks one Sunday,
And it was love at first sight
Between Larry and Billy.
As a matter of fact,
They ignored me the rest of the afternoon,
Getting along as if they had known each other
For years.
After that, we saw a lot of Billy.
Billy was so happy for us.
On a particularly chilly rainy Sunday,
Billy had us over for a late brunch
And movie.
We're sitting in front of this roaring fire,
Billy's watching us,
And says…
Why don't you two get married?
We both looked at him horror stricken,
As neither of us believe men should marry.
But the way Billy talked about it,
It sounded perfectly wonderful.

It wouldn't be a marriage,
Just a commitment ceremony.
Billy said we could have it performed
On his terrace, with the Hudson
For a backdrop.
We could invite just our closest friends
Who would support us in our decision.
So, after discussing it at length,
We decided why the Hell not.
Larry was not quite as comfortable
With the idea as I was, but we made a date
For Sunday April 25.
Billy wanted to pay for everything,
And we invited 12 friends.
Billy made the terrace an absolute
Spring wonderland.
There were huge terracotta pots
With trained Fiscus trees that had thousands
Of peach, yellow, and white blooms.

To keep it private,
The caterer set everything up and
Then left until the ceremony was finished.
What was the most beautiful were the words.

Larry to Drew

Our friend, Reverend Lambert,
An Episcopal Minister,
Performed the ceremony for us.

LARRY "Once I merely existed
On a non-descript plane
Drifting through a life I can only
Describe as beige."

"There were pastel accents,
But there were no facets or edges,
Only flat surfaces…
And round corners.
No fire…no outrageous colors.
The lock on my life was beginning to strain,
Keeping this heart bound in chains of loneliness.
But as swift as a meteor,
A comet named Drew crashed
Through the atmosphere of my life.
Yes, this beautiful mass of loving energy
Roared into my being,
Grasping the key to that lock,
And I who was once a bland participant in life,
Am now an incredibly happy man,
Gratefully basing his life on someone else's, yes
On someone else's existence.
I've seen before my very eyes

A man, a mere mortal if you will,
Meld magnificence into this heart.
This heart willing to take
This private, but none-the-less
Sacred vow.
As I read this to you…
Please look into my eyes".

(He didn't have to worry; I plan to spend much of my life
Gazing into those eyes.)

"Dear Drew,"
As long as I can open my eyes to you
In the morning,
I have all there is to cherish in this world.
As long as I feel the warmth
Of your breath on my cheek,
The beat of your heart,
The rustling of your being,
While living from room to room,
Then I know all is well in my world,
Our world."

"Before my eyes
I've seen you challenge me
To love, to live, and to be fulfilled.
And as long as I have you,
I am alive.
With all my heart Drew
I love you and not that I'm worthy,

But I humbly ask you
To share all my days,
All of my time,
Every precious second,
I am earthbound,
As my heart's mate,
Soul mate,
And companion.
Will you be my partner in life, Drew?"

As I gazed into those breath-taking green eyes,
I had to swallow to make sure I had a voice,
And reassure myself this was not a dream.

DREW "Yes, Larry,

    For as long as you want me
    I will be your companion for life."

(Then it was my turn, and after hearing Larry,
I thought maybe he should be a writer too.)

"My beautiful Larry,
I am overwhelmed and amazed at all
The beautiful words and phrases I
Have just heard.
Although I'm a professional writer,
I could never have written anything
As beautiful and eloquent,
So let me begin by saying,
That I too found my life becoming

Just an existence.
Although my work was fulfilling,
There was a large piece of the puzzle missing.
The part that would make me complete,
That would lift me,
Help me to soar,
To realize complete and true happiness.
The funny thing is,
I knew it was out there.
I just didn't know if I would
Ever own it.
And as the puzzle has been completed,
It has emerged as a beautiful painting of life,
You and I together."

"In this crazy world it is so rare
For two people, especially two gay
People to find a love so passionate
And full, and it seems we have."

"Although I can't guarantee you perfection,
I can guarantee that I will try to
Make your life as perfect as possible.
Please allow me the room for mistakes"

"So I humbly ask you
To share all my time and days,
Every season, month, and second,
As we ride on the hands of the clock of life.
I ask you to share my life, my wealth,

My sorrow, my joy and my heart,
To partner with me on this wonderful
Journey through this magnificent life.
After all, aren't you the reason it's magnificent?
Will you share my life with me Larry?"

LARRY "I stand here knowing there are people in
The world who shall never have the chance
To love as I have. For that reason and
Because I love you so much,
I will share your life with you, Drew."

And as you can guess, we kissed each other.
Our friends and the minister all cried,
As we did.
And then we spent the rest of the day
Sharing ourselves with our wonderful friends.

Billy told me the reason he's not involved
With anyone is because he's waiting for
Someone like us.

A Day In The Life

After I've adjusted my head from the banging
Of what sounds like Big Ben,
I open one eye at a time and look over
To see if Larry is still there,
And when I see that gorgeous head of chestnut hair,
Life starts.

I always cuddle up to his back
And reach my arm over and gently prick his nipple.
Then my hand travels south
And if there is any "hard activity…"
…well, we don't leave the bed right away.

It's amazing but we've been together
Well over a year,
And the lovemaking just gets
Better, and better, and better, and…
Well, you get the picture.
Thank God we have two bathrooms!

Since I work from home I'm not in a hurry,
But Larry has to be on Wall Street.
So I take a whiz,
Jump in the shower,
Shave,
And dry the feathers quickly.
The coffee's on a timer and ready

By the time I get out of the shower.
I take Larry a cup
And start breakfast.

The blind could almost time us.
I get the papers,
Lay them on the table,
And Larry comes in ravenous.
Since he likes to read the news,
I watch Good Morning America
While he reads.

It's about the time I'm wishing
He would get the hell out and go to work.
I can't get started with my writing
Until I have absolute quiet and no distractions.
He's not due at the office until 9:00 A.M.,
And by 8:30 I'm at my desk,
About thirty seconds after he's gone.
My desk is in the library at the window
Overlooking Central Park;
The incredible view where I give birth
To my characters.

Although we're madly in love,
We realize the importance of our respective
Careers and success…once after talking,
We realize our success adds so much to who we are.

I suppose now would be a good time
To tell you about Lawrence Barton Jr.

Wasp old family probably traced to the Mayflower
Senior is the scion of the family
Expectations run high for Junior
Continue in the shoes and success
Harvard, Wharton, introductions
Membership in all the right clubs
The one's that won't let me be a member
Unless there's 8 zeros to invest.
Then the mat rolls out.
There's lines to be towed
Rules to follow though not written down
Larry's the great white hope
Excelled at everything
Debutantes thrown at him.
Senior wants to know why no wedding bells
Junior explains, he's waiting for
A Jackie O.
Produce the proper heirs, etc.
Junior's secret is he's gay
Big no no in Senior's world
His too really
Of course now he's met me...
Uh oh!

Apple cart's about to be upset
Larry has a cousin who is light in the loafers
Old Senior finds it disgusting.
Cuz fooled 'em all and made a big fortune
In a junk bond house
It really frosts Senior's balls.
He's grateful his son is "straight"

Junior has done his part
He's dated women for appearances
Slept with men on the down low
Increased firm's business 28%
Star of the firm
Meets up with Cuz for Fire Island fun
Senior would ruin Junior if he ever suspected
Junior's resigned to a life of
Quiet desperation
One day it will all be his
Senior has a dirty secret
Her name is Ruth Lawrence
She wanted Senior to marry her
He had her conveniently "put away"
Junior is itching to break the mold.
He's held back by fear
So Junior meets me and he's
Thinking about that mold
And what mold can do to a wall
Or a building if not taken care of

Larry's office is at Number 38 Wall Street.
We're meeting for lunch at Delmonico's
Junior wants me to see his office

You'd swear Stanford White designed
The building, and Rose Cummings the interiors.
The first time I met him for lunch
I was visibly impressed.
His office has green marble floors,

A coffered ceiling from a summer home in England,
The paneling is hand carved walnut
With English antique brass hardware.
As legend has it,
His huge mahogany elaborately carved desk
Was from J.P. Morgan's Yacht, Corsair,

Not only are there marble accents and cornices,
But a Carrera marble fireplace.
The place reeks of money…old and new.
Concealed behind the paneling
Is a completely stocked bar,
And to the left of that
Is a state-of-the-art stereo system,
Which Larry has in constant use,
You hear a lot of Sondheim.
When Daddy's not around

Larry's carrying on in the family business,
Making sure that portfolios of some of the
Oldest families in the country continue to bulge.
He likes his career, in fact, he loves his career
And that's what's important.
I have no head when it comes to investments,
Transactions or bonds or leverage…
Any of those terms I hear him use.
When he discusses them with me,
I smile and nod
And act as if I do understand.
A little aside…I gave Larry a hundred thousand dollars

To invest…
It took him a year, but he turned it into a million
I am overjoyed he understands writing
And he will read a piece I've written
And intelligently discuss it with me.
I love my career and that also is important.
I rarely if ever have a block when I'm writing;
Maybe that's because I do it on a daily basis without fail.
I sit at my desk and go at a straight four-hour clip,
Stop for a little lunch and continue.
If I'm on a roll and shooting for a deadline,
I go until it's finished or I'm exhausted.
And God-bless Larry, he understands.
The phone calls keep us together,
I'll hear from him about 10:30 in the morning
And if I'm in a creative mood, I don't answer,
Which he understands
On the other hand, his secretary Sarah
Let's me know when he's tied up
And makes sure he calls me.

Being a member, of the family,
Larry is able to leave around 4:30.
We have a ritual that almost every day
We meet somewhere for afternoon tea
And walk home together
It amazes me that we can find so much to discuss
On a daily basis.
We absolutely adore the city
And always find a little surprise

In the architecture.
One day we want to do a coffee table book
On some of the really interesting small
Buildings in New York.

For tea we split it up between
Woods on 37th, The Russian Tea Room, or
The Palm Court at the Plaza Hotel.
When we are daring, it's the Wollman Rink
In Central Park.
Usually we wander home and end up there
Around 6:30 P.M.

Larry and I have a little philosophy about money,
And that is...spend it to have a good time!
And we do...but we also give a lot to charity
And we're both involved in community service.
We go out four or five times a week.
Our secret, is that we dine early...usually 7,
And then go to a party or the opening of
A show...I know we see everything on Broadway
Off Broadway...near Broadway...and sometimes we
Hit small theaters out of town.

Larry has rented out his Park Avenue Co-op
So, we have filled our apartment with artwork
Blooming from a source of new artists we love.
The house will never make Architectural Digest
But we're not trying to impress anyone.

In the study, library, den, pick a name.
We have committed the unpardonable decorating sin!

We have a pair of massaging reclining chairs
That are comfortable as hell, and we don't give a
Damn whether they are acceptable or not.
We like them, spend many hours in them, and
Realize that much of our conversation emanates from
Those chairs…so take that Mario Buatta!

This is a typical sharing time…
Our favorite day is Sunday…we absolutely never
Plan one thing on Sunday except to be together.
That morning starts with rich fresh imported
Coffee from a little shop in the Village.
If it's chilly we stay in bed letting the sunlight stream in
To warm us and entertain us as we watch the activity
On the Hudson come alive.

If it's warm,
We go out on the terrace with the Times
And just stay quiet and read the paper.
That's when we also plan all of these trips
To those outrageous places in the travel section.

Around 11 it's time for a bagel after which
We shower and get dressed and head off "auctioning."
We love to hit the auction galleries on the East Side.
There's a lot of junk, but mostly treasure.
It's amazing who you see when they auction a
Celebrity estate.

When Gloria Swanson's things came up, you
Couldn't get in
We saw the line, but since we had a friend
Who works there, I went back down the block and
Called her.
She promptly took us through the back door.
It was a waste of time since we didn't see
Anything we would die over.

The magic with us is that we simultaneously
Zero in on the same object at the same time.
A piece of crystal, a silver object.
We've practically furnished the house at
Davis Park with things from the Doyle Gallery.

After doing all the galleries, usually around 6
We head for Jim McMullen's for chicken pot pie.
Then it's to the corner video store to rent a
Film…and home.

The blight on our beautiful Sundays is that
Larry usually hears from his family and they
Pretend our lifestyle doesn't exist.
They also make no bones about the fact I
Don't exist.

It's not easy because Larry is from an old family
And they just don't understand "gay" people.
That's okay, because I don't understand prejudice.
What makes all of our days special,
Is that we love and adore each other.

Larry allows me to be me with him,
To share everything I have with him
And he shares all he has with me,
We have each other, we have our love,
Our lives, our careers, but most of all
We have these beautiful days together.

Nothing's Perfect

Don't get me wrong
I sure as hell don't want to
Sound like Pollyanna.
Although our relationship is as close to
Perfect as possible,
It's not...
Larry is not a saint
And although I've been nicknamed Teresa
I am no saint either.
In fact, we fight...quietly I might add
And Larry does things that piss me off.
While I'm sure I must do one or two
Little things that irritates him...
Things are for the most part
Extraordinary.
His biggest gripe is that I don't
Wipe the basin after I brush my teeth...
Like I said, no one's perfect...

To look at Larry you would think this
Man is walking perfection without flaw...
Just simply not true...
He farts...
And when I say fart...
I mean big old smelly farts
That shake the windows.
He's had every test imaginable

And he's healthy…
He just farts!
Some of these farts are so bad
You would swear something crawled up
His ass and died…

They're worse when he's eaten Mexican food
Especially beans…Those farts are so bad
They could knock a buzzard off
A shit wagon at fifty yards…
It wouldn't be so bad…
Except sometimes when we're in bed
He will come on very tender
Maybe a little snuggle
To get me worked up…
And then he'll let out a huge
Window shaking earthquake sized fart
And hold the damn covers over my head…
That may sound funny
But one day I swear I'm going to pass out…
Can you see the headline in the POST…
"MAN ASPHYXIATED BY KILLER FART"…male lover
Held without bail…soon to be a mini-series.

Of course, I get tickled and then Larry
Gets tickled and we can't stop laughing
And there goes making love.
It's hard to imagine that something
That smelly could escape from something
That gorgeous…and his body is …gorgeous!

Except for one thing…
On his back…left side…just below
The shoulder is this great big
Old ugly red mole…
And it has three hairs growing out of it.
Three kinky black hairs…
And I've named them…
Myrtle, Ethel…and Thelma…
I want to cut them…but Larry says no…
Something about superstition…

We eat most of our meals out…
That's why God made New York City…
So you can dine out.
One just has to compromise…
And Larry feels his mission in life
Is to get me to try every obnoxious
Creature that can be boiled, baked
Broiled, sautéed, fried, or grilled.

And if the restaurant is Asian…
So much the better.
I am just not as adventurous as Larry…
And the hind legs of a cricket in
Chili sauce ain't my idea of dinner…
But I try…
Most odd things on menus have
Strange textures…

Once we had dinner in Korea Town,
And Larry asked me to try something

I couldn't pronounce...
It looked like marbles and tasted
As I assume snot would taste if cooked...
It turned out to be fish eyes in a
Garlic butter sauce...
I tried to be brave...
But turned sort of green
Ran to the restroom and lost it.
He thought it was funny.
I didn't speak to him for two days...

I will try things, but I'm
Careful...
I have to admit,
I'm a little set in my ways...

That's just the way things are
And I know what I like
And things usually work out
When I follow my instincts and my heart
And my tastes...
That includes movies...
Larry loves foreign movies...
Any nationality...
Any story line
Whether it be a classic or
Contemporary...
History or a love story...
And I must admit I have tried...
I guess being a writer

I can create stories and characters
In my head...
Just call me jaded.

Larry got interested in films
Through his job...
One of the international businesses
He puts his clients in,
Is Investing in syndicates that
Provide funding for films worldwide.
They actually hope for a flop
But Larry asks for a synopsis
And a cast breakdown before he
Invests...and his instincts are
Incredible...he's right on 90%
Of the time...

I usually enjoy the French and English
Films...
But...
When it gets to
The Turkish love stories...
Polish war histories...
Well, I hope you get the picture...

It's called a compromise for love...
I'm sure Larry hates being dragged to
Off, off-Broadway to see some of
The productions I like...
I will stress again

The important aspect of all of this
Is not whether it's perfect or not…
We do many things together
Because we love each other…
And when love is at its best
I believe for me
That this is fairly close
To perfection…

Little Ol' Me

Maybe you are,
Maybe you aren't...
That is asking yourself this question...
We know about Larry...
How gorgeous he is,
How kind and patient and giving he is...
But what about little ol' me?
What's he like?
Well you sort of have an idea...
But what does he look like?
What does he think?
What's he for?
What's he against?
In other words...
You want to know...
What, when, where, why, how, and who?

I will do my best to tell you...
But briefly...
I'm slightly modest...
And shy...

If I used one word to describe
Myself and my life...
Let's see...
It would be...yes...
Fortunate...

That's what I am,
Fortunate.
I feel I am because
No matter what has happened
In my life,
I have always landed on my feet…
There's always been a feeling
Of it's going to be alright…
Don't panic…
And it usually works that way.

I was born in the early fifties
In Manhattan in Greenwich Village.
We lived in a wonderful building
At 30 Christopher Street,
Right in the heart of the West Village.
My mother was a professional volunteer,
And my father made deals…
Never worked a day in his life…
Our family was very small,
As my Mom and Dad
Were both only children.
There was always plenty of money
And my folks loved me like crazy.

They planned things constantly…
We went to musicals and plays…
Concerts…museums…restaurants…
Where there was life to behold…
My family beheld it…

And the parties...
I think my folks entertained
At least once a week...
All kinds of people from all walks of life...

We had this sign on our apartment door...
"If you have hatred or feel bigotry for
 Another human being, then you have knocked
 On the wrong door!"
At one of their parties
You might find a Broadway star getting
A plate of food for a waiter from Lindy's,
Or a Congressman discussing politics
With a fabric cutter from the garment district...
I was fortunate because our apartment
Was happy and a safe haven from the "grind"
Of the big city.

Because of my upbringing,
I was happy most of the time...
If I wasn't or just a little unsettled,
My folks noticed and it was discussed...
My father had the insight
To notice I was different.
Being very intelligent...
My folks tested me...
That is to see what I liked
In the world...
And once they knew,
They encouraged me in all my endeavors.

They knew I had a passion for reading
So I had a liberal allowance for books…
On all kinds of subjects…
I loved the theater…any theater…
And although it was indulgent,
They took me to everything…
On, off, off-off, near, and far Broadway!
One thing I received from my father was
The love of fine clothing…
And he taught me about different styles
Of men's suits, the cut, the fabrics,
And made sure I had the best.

I had dozens of friends as a young man
And our apartment looked like a social club…
I was a gawky teenager spawned from
A Chubby child…
I had acne and had to wear glasses,
Had two left feet…but I could do three
Things very well…
I could write, and I did for the school paper…
I could dance my ass off and did…
And swim like a trout…and won about every
Trophy my school and the state offered.

When I turned sixteen
I became a swan,
I had a good physique from all the swimming…
White creamy smooth skin after acne…
A sense of humor…thank you Jesus…

Perfect white teeth...not one cavity...thank you Crest...
Five feet ten inches of good health...
The respect of my fellow students
And the feeling I was loved...
I was again fortunate,
Because I knew what I wanted to do...
Except I never planned to grow up...
I was going to be a writer...

I knew that since I was twelve...
I kept two journals...
Once was a record of actual events in my life
As they happened...
The other a fictionalized version...
It was steamy, full of sex, corruption,
And violence...
I knew enough interesting people...
That if I was stuck for a plot point
Or needed a fascinating character...
I would call one of my parent's
Theater friends and get help...
I called my journal...
The Love of Lust...
I didn't tell my folks about the journal...
Instead I asked a family friend in publishing
To read it...he did...and...
Published it...
It got to be number 13 on the best seller list
Before it dropped off...
I also wrote it under the pen name of

Miller Stone…
I came home one day from school
And there's a copy on the coffee table…
My father is pretending anger…
Tells me he knows the whole scam…
Breaks up laughing and tells me its
A damn good book…
He found out when the bank credited
My $72,000 royalty check to his account…
He loved it…

The only thing I didn't deal with
As a teenager…was my sexuality…
I was ashamed of being gay…
I wanted to produce a family and
Children just as my parents had done…
Now I knew my feelings were different…
And I really became aware of that
When I was on the swim team…
I was physically drawn to the beauty
Of the well … developed male body…
And male bonding and touching was a necessity…
But there was no way I was going to
Have sex with another man…
Ever until the first time it happened…
I have to back up though…
I was deflowered at fourteen
By a very amorous nineteen-year-old girl
Who lived in my building…
She had a brother who was on the swim team

And she would come to our meets...
I should mention...
God was good to me below the waist...
And of course, I had a large bulge
In my bathing suit.
One day I was in the basement
Getting the laundry for my mom...
Next thing I know Sandra is there...
She's striking up a conversation
Which gets around to sex...
The next thing you know...
She's got me aroused...
And well a stiff dick has no conscience
And off to her apartment we go...
I liked it...
But something was missing...
At sixteen I found out what was missing...
My sexuality exploded like a bomb...
I was constantly horny...
And damn near wore out my hand
Jerking off several time a day
I had my first crush on Glen Barret,
A kid in my class...
He was the school rebel...
Not a hood...just didn't take shit
Off anyone...
Street and book smart...
We hit it off immediately
And spent an enormous amount of time together...
He adored my parents and hated his...

Because they were drunks and fought constantly…
One time after school…
Glen asked if he could come home
With me and stay for a while…
He was upset and I sensed it.
He was quiet…
Soon I got him to talk
And then great torrents of pain escaped from him…
His father had been jailed the night before…
He almost killed Glen's mother and
Glen called the police…
They found coke and drugs in the house and took his
Father to jail…
After they left…
His mother threw him out…
Since the father was the paycheck
He spent the night,
And of course, he slept in my bed.
He fell right to sleep and rolled over
Close to me.
The feel of his skin next to mine
Was the most incredible feeling I had ever had.
I rolled over and went to sleep too.

I woke up about four in the morning
To find Glen cuddled up to me like a baby…
His hand was on my crotch and I had
This enormous …
He was fast asleep and I didn't know
What to do…

I thought if I responded he might get mad...
So I slowly turned until I was facing him...
I just lay there staring at his face...
Then he gently opened his eyes...
Kissed me on the forehead...
And started slowly taking my underwear off...

I don't know where or how or who
Taught Glen what he knew...
But he was incredible...
I had never experienced anything
Like that in my life...
We finished and Glen went back to sleep...
I stayed awake until it was time to go to school.
Glen stayed at my house and slept in...
I don't remember that day of school,
All I thought about was Glen...

He stayed at my house for six weeks...
By then I was hopelessly in love...
How did Glen feel about this?
He wasn't sure...
He knew he was straight...
Still had feelings for girls...
But something happened between us...
Finally, Glen went back to his house...
His father got out of jail and beat the
Shit out of him...
As he was a minor, they shipped him
Off to military school...

I'm not sure the reason,
But he was forbidden to talk to me
Or see me…

Thank God you have stamina when you're 16
And that healing is faster…
I did see Glen six months later…
I ran into him at the movies with
His girlfriend Brenda…
The good that came out of it was
That my mother figured out what
Was going on…and could feel my pain.
She was gentle and asked me if I had
Strong feelings for boys…
She was so gentle that I told her the truth…
Now knowing what to expect…
What I received was support.
Both of my folks sat me down…
And while they were looking forward
To grandchildren,
They were more concerned that I be happy.
Furthermore,
They said if I felt I needed therapy
They would gladly arrange it…
I said no…I loved them and I was happy…
I really was…

In summer we travelled all over the
Country and the world…
So it was no surprise

When I decided to go to school
To study journalism
At Columbia University...
Being the bright student I was...
I enrolled at 17...
And bankrolled it myself
With the royalties from the book...
I also decided to live at home...
I had been treated as an adult with trust
Most of my life...
And really loved my parents...
If I stayed over with a date
At their house, they understood.
If I had a date stay over,
They understood that also...
I had flings and affairs,
But no one lived up to Glen...

During spring break,
I was going to meet my parents in Miami
And from there we were going on to Key West...
They were flying in from Bermuda
And I was coming in from the "Apple."
It's still very hard to talk about...
As simple as this...
Their plane crashed and burned...
There were no survivors...
And I thank God everyday
I had them as long as I did and
That they taught me so much...

How to love…how to live…
AND IT'S ALRIGHT TO BE ME!

I had not yet turned 18,
And technically since there were no
Other relatives…I could have been
A ward of the court…
But again, because I knew powerful people…
I was allowed to keep the apartment
And raise myself…

After thoroughly searching the apartment…
I found the will…
Everything was left to me and
Parson's School of Design…
I loved my old man
But he spent a lot of the money…
After the taxes and Parson's
I ended up with about $250,000.00
Not only that, to insure my future
It turns out my father had bought
2500 shares of a company called Polaroid
And 2500 shares of Xerox.
You know what they're worth today?
It sure made my life easy…
Because I could go to school and write…
Thank you, Mom and Dad.
There was one more thing I found
In their safe deposit box…

A letter addressed to me...
It's my favorite thing in the world
And I want to share it with you...

Dear Drew,

We're not sure when you will receive this letter. Whether you're young or old. It doesn't matter. This is a tribute to the finest son any parents could ever have been blessed with. You have always been such a source of pride for us. Light is what we think about when we think of you. So open, so loving, such joy to be around. Yes, as parents we couldn't have asked for more.

The greatest joy we ever had was to watch you sleep. To see you gently move and gurgle. Like an angel. If we never gave you anything, we hope you know you were loved and adored beyond our wildest dreams. And if you ever had any doubt about us loving you when we found out you were gay, forget it. We want you to know that it's not important how or who you love; what's important is that you know how to love and allow yourself to be loved in return.

We know you're feeling grief over our leaving...don't son. Be happy that we had a wonderful life together. We enjoyed an incredible love and so much beautiful time together...and Son, we wish all of that for you. And one more thing...if you're ever in trouble or sad, think of this letter and the two people that were so fortunate as to have been the parents and friend of the most wonderful child imaginable.

We Love You,
Mom and Dad

Thank you for letting me share this with you.
I have a couple of other things to tell you about me
I ended up about 5 feet 10 inches tall.
My hair is auburn brown
And when I'm in the sun for a few days,
It turns a nice shade of copper…
My eyes are blue,
Not azure or Caribbean, but blue.
I have a slim medium build…
I walk and watch my diet most of the time…
There are slips occasionally.
I am considered attractive
Rather than handsome…
But I believe my insides are
Beautiful because I work at it…
I am happy to be alive…
And even when it's at its worst
Life is good,
Because I learned early
That the bad times will pass…
I'm rich and don't apologize for it…
I love my success and work at it…
I love my apartment…
My clothes…
Manhattan and everything that goes with it…
I love my friends…
I'm a good friend too…

And most of all,
I love being in love…
Moving right along…

Our First Fight

I have a tendency to rock the boat even
When the water is smooth, and,
Without batting an eye
I fully accept the guilt and responsibility
Of starting our first fight…
Even though we had one hell of a time making up.

It all started when I had a particularly testy day
I was really pissed…mad at the world…
His majesty the baby was not getting his way…
I had a writing block with a deadline due…
And I was looking for bear!
That was me.

Larry is rarely if ever anything
But a bundle of joy and all smiles.
He prefers to keep anger to himself
Or work it out on the racquet ball court…
We are always supportive of each other
And you'd think we live in "Never Never Land!"
So, this same day,
Larry comes home very edgy
Because I wouldn't meet him
At the Plaza for tea… (it's one of our rituals)
He tells me a certain company he's
Heavily invested client's money in
Has fallen 18 points on the market…

Now it's a target for greenmail.
That's serious for him and I should
Have forgotten my petty bitch
And tried to be there for him,
But I wasn't.

So here's what happened…

I said,   "Before you say anything, I just wasn't
            in the mood to drag my ass down to the
            Plaza, so please forgive me."

He said,   "Consider yourself forgiven…I needed to
            see you and could have used your company..
            because it was a tough day on the market today."

I said,   "Me too, I couldn't write shit, I'm bored stiff,
            so let's get dressed, get the hell out of here,
            and have a wonderful, rich fattening dinner."

He said,   "I'd really like to take a shower, have a drink,
            order in, and share some Chinese on the terrace
            with my reason for being."

Now if I hadn't been such an asshole, I would have thought
about the beautiful thing he just said. But no…so,

I said,   "I've been cooped up all day and I want to go out…
            we don't have to stay too long. How about the
            Ginger Man?"

He said,   "I'm really beat, but maybe being out will cheer me up…Ginger Man's fine. What a day! The economy's in the toilet. I hope Reagan's next term is better."

I said,   "Reagan again…are you crazy? We need a democrat who supports the arts. Someone like a Ted Kennedy."

He said,   "Did you say Kennedy? Did I hear correctly? Drew, you amaze me. You're just too smart to say something like that. Kennedy's not strong enough…he'll never live down that accident…Hell, he wants to give more to the poor and screw the rich at the same time."

Understand, I don't have an active interest in politics, but I was itching for a fight to get over my writers block so I opened my big mouth and……

I said,   "That's a crock of shit and since you spend the better part of the day reading three newspapers, and you don't even do the crossword puzzle, but really read the damn things, you should know better!"

He said,   "Drew, this isn't like you, are you on something?"

I said,   "What! You know damn well I'm not on anything, nor have I even had my first drink of the day.

	Just because I finally voice a political opinion, and I'm on something? Well fuck you and the horse you rode in on!"
He said,	"Now wait a damn minute…just hold it Drew. We don't talk to each other this way. Are you sure nothing is wrong?
I said,	"No, Goddamit, nothing's wrong. I just happen to want my opinion respected."
He said,	"I have always respected you, and when you have an opinion worth respecting, I will, but not when you make statements out of anger. Now, can we drop it and have dinner?"

Wow, was he getting formal or what? The poor man was actually practicing self-control to keep from breaking my neck, which I deserved, but…

I said,	"Listen Mr. Wall Street, I am a respected writer, and people pay a lot of money to read what I've written, and the magazines I write for are not exactly schlock, so there!"

Wouldn't you just know he had a hurt look and was ready to take all the blame and let me off the hook

He said,	"Drew, I'm sorry, I shouldn't have said that, so let me apologize now, because I really didn't mean it."

Now I could have let it drop right there, but I had my dander up and somebody was going to pay; and in a way I liked the way the adrenalin was making me feel, and besides it was time I tested him to see how far I could push him, just to prove he really loved me. It's just a shame somebody wasn't there to kick my ass.

I said, "Of course you meant it. People will always tell truth when they're angry, so you can order Chinese or Czechoslovakian and stuff it up your ass on the terrace and give the whole park a show."

He said, "Drew, I don't talk to you like that and you're not going to talk to me that way either."

I said, " I just did, and who the hell are you, my father?"

He said, "No, I'm not your father, I'm the person who loves you, and I'd like an apology, and an end to this conversation before it goes so far it can never be repaired."

I said, "When Hell freezes over."

Now if this sounds out of character for Drew to be like this, it is. You see, with all this love, I'm still insecure…everyone I've ever loved has left me. I'm in therapy, but a little piece of me still doesn't think I'm loved enough…so once in a while I need to test it. It's like a little demon in me takes over and turns me into another person…a mean…bitch, which I'm not.

He said,   "You need to cool off, so I'm going for a walk, and when I get back, if you still want to, we can go to dinner."

I said,   "Don't you dare go out that door."

Barbara Stanwyck never said it better, believe me.

He said,   "Drew, don't give me orders, and yes, I'm getting the hell out of here for a few minutes. I've never seen you like this, and it scares the Hell out of me."

I said,   "Well fine, a little problem arises and you run like a chicken with its head cut off.

He slammed out through that door…I have never seen him so angry, and I'm trying to figure out what the hell is the matter with me, but I still had to keep the drama going, So after he had been gone a few minutes, I went to the Works, a neighborhood gay bar where they show old classic movies. I ordered a stiff drink and settled back to watch a few minutes of *Imitation of Life*. When it got to the part about the mother dying and the daughter flinging herself on the coffin, well I lost it. I realized I had been watching the film for an hour. I was hungry, a little drunk, and suddenly afraid that I had damaged my relationship beyond repair…
I rush into the apartment with my head hung in shame. He's not there.

I sit down frantically and try to figure out
Where he might be.
Another hour passes and still no Larry…
It's getting close to eleven
So, I start calling friends…
Finally, I reach Mike McCarthy
And tell him about the fight,
He reads me the riot act
And tells me what an asshole I really am.
Mike reminds me about the wonderful
Man in my life,
And how perfect our relationship has been…
Suddenly cold dead fear registers in me…

Almost in hysterics,
I run out on the street
To start looking for him,
But I wouldn't know where to look
So I waited…
And finally about midnight
I heard the turn of his key in the lock…
I held my breath as he came in the living room.

He looked at me with those
Gorgeous green eyes…
Before I could say anything he said…

"I went to the bar on the corner
And had a drink to try and sort out
Just what happened…

I was angry at you and went to
A double feature.
The second movie was *Terms of Endearment*
And when it came to the scene where
Emma's dying and her son still won't
Say I love you to her,
I had the most incredible
Bout of sadness I have ever felt…
And then I thought that if you died,
And we hadn't straightened this out,
How sad it would be for the two of us…
Then he said for me not to say anything…
He put his hand under my chin,
Drew my face up so he could look in my eyes,

And said,

"Drew, since you've been in my life, I've never been
so happy…you're good for me, good to me…I'm not
sure what happened tonight…I know it scared the hell
out of me. If it was my fault, I'm sorry…really sorry;
Because consciously I would never knowingly do
anything to hurt you or make you angry. I feel it was
a matter of two guys asserting some macho bullshit
into a situation that didn't event call for it. I was in
a lousy mood and obviously you were too, and we
both reacted to the other's hostility for the days
events. Please let's don't ever do this, because I
can't stand being angry with you…and I was for a while.
I'm not blame-less, you had a bad day also and I could

have been a little more giving. I promise I will try harder. More than I can ever tell you, more than I can ever show you, I love you and thank you for what you've done for my life. If it's okay, I would like to pretend tonight didn't happen!"

Then he gives me the biggest hug and kiss
You can imagine,
And I'm feeling like such a jerk
And he knows it
And spends the rest of the night
Showing me
Just how much he loves me.

The next morning, I get up early and watch the Sun find its way over the buildings on 5th Ave. And as I feel those rays warm me. I say, thank You God, for I am blessed.

IF

If you didn't love me,
I'm not sure I would be complete,
If you didn't love me,
I'm not sure I would shine as brightly as I do,
If you didn't love me,
I'm not sure I would be living my life so fully,
But you do,
And please don't stop,
Because if you did,
If you did...
I don't even want to think about it.

If you're eyes weren't so green,
If you're body weren't so hard,
If your hands weren't so gentle,
If your sense of humor wasn't there,
If your mouth wasn't so luscious,
If your lovemaking wasn't so damn passionate,
If your essence wasn't so rare,
If you weren't here,
I would be so lost,

If I didn't see you in the morning,

Would I see so clearly?
If I didn't know you were next to me at night,

Would I sleep with such peace?
If you didn't have such a knack for giving life detail,

Would my life have as many facets as a prism?
The answer to all these questions is NO.

But I don't worry and live within this land of IF.
I know you love me,
I know your eyes are green,
I know my light shines bright,
My life has much more meaning,
You are there,
You add those delicacies and the subtleties,
They can't be defined other than to say,
I can compare it to making a brilliant sauce,
It's the spicing that when it is perfect,
The sauce passes from good to sublime,

I find my heart is filled with awe and contentment,
Because your love has filled me like pages of a book,
And you are all I need to know to experience who I am,
Now that I am me,
Because of you,
But If there was no you,
It seems doubtful there would be much of me as I am today.
It's you I'm so aware of!

Sunday in the Park with Drew and Larry

I suppose some would call us insane…
Two people as delirious as we are
How amazing…
Things feel different
And taste different
And look different…
The joy you can find in an old tree
The cracks that form an etching in a rock
The swans that perform a ballet in the lake
I have never seen such a collection
Or more beautiful people
Than in Central Park today
Being in love certainly changes one's perspective
On many things,
But especially life.
I don't even have to analyze it
To tell you that for the first time
In a long time
There is absolutely nothing wrong
With any aspect of my life.

What a difference to smell the roses
They really do squirt perfume on you.
What a difference in a sunset
The magentas and golds
Such an awareness and openness

About all the things that are important
And being aware of your body
And how it feels
It's almost as if there's a gentle tingling
And Jesus!
When he touches me
Or when I see him walk in a room
There's a tiny gasp of air that escapes my lips
From excitement
And how incredible to be in Manhattan
In this park
With this man
On this sunny day
With just a touch of briskness
To remind you winter's not ready to let go for spring.
That two people can find their own world
On this eight-foot patch of grass
Among a million other people
And to walk for hours that seem only like minutes
Through Strawberry Fields
While the Dakota looms over our shoulders
Like a silent sentry standing guard
Protecting our welfare
Do you notice that no one seems to mind
That we are two men…
Two men in love!

Billy Rutger

Before it's said and done
We'd like to think every day and everything
Is one big picnic...
It ain't!
Although it's not very loud or violent,
Larry and I do fight occasionally (once I wrote about)
So what else is new...we like making up.
Our strength and faith have never waivered
In each other
And thank God
Because we had a devastating crisis
In our life...
Our very best friend in the Village
Whose apartment was where we had our ceremony
Was recently diagnosed with the Big "A",
And in this case
"A" sure don't mean apple...
Pure and simple...AIDS

Aids is probably the most horrid
Putrid, Filthy word ever said
Worse than motherfucker
And that's what this disease is,
A Motherfucker
Because it's killing my beautiful friends
Ending beautiful lives
Of people that only want to create...

Add brilliance to the world…
It's one thing to fight
But it's hell when you don't know how
And what you're fighting.

Billy was the kind of person
That would walk into a room
And work it!
Before the night was over
He'd know everyone and something about them
He had a smile that would dazzle…
He gossiped humorously but I can't
Remember him ever saying anything
Mean or hurtful about anyone.

Billy and I met right out of college
At a friend's house in the village…
I was going to be a writer
And he was going to own an antique store
That way,
He knew he would meet people that would care
About beautiful things…about life
People who could appreciate the time and effort
It took to create a piece of Louis XIV furniture.
Fortunately, our dreams came true.

As friends we were inseparable
And once thought we might be in love
But it didn't click
So, we settled on glued-to-the hip friendship.

We've been through everything together
Love affairs…heart breaks
Deaths in our families;
All of my family is dead,
So, Billy it is.
We spent all of our holidays together
Going on buying trips to Europe for the store
I would do research…a way to write it off.
Billy trusted my taste and asked my approval
On many of his purchases…
I let him read anything I wrote first
Because if it was shit, he'd tell me
And then tell me why
And damn, he was usually right on the money.

He adored Larry immediately
And even told me he was envious.
Larry adored Billy from the very first also
So it was easy for the three of us to travel
Together on holidays
If we had a disagreement
We'd both call Billy…
He usually had the common sense we needed
To solve whatever the problem we
Needed help with.

Billy had a few short-lived romances,
But just never found "Mr. Right".
I never could figure out why
Because he was so handsome…

Flashing blue eyes…
Auburn hair
And a fabulous body…
Of course he hit the gym and jogged daily.

He lived in the most wonderful space…
On the roof of a warehouse two blocks
North of the Village at 16th & Hudson.
The view was magical…overlooking the river.
Billy stored antique shipments for himself
And other dealers in the warehouse below
Through his cleverness of obtaining more
And more leases on the space…
Eventually he leased about eighty percent
Of the building and when it came up
For sale, he bought it.
Once he owned the building,
He built a three-bedroom bungalow on the roof

Complete with a swimming pool and terrace…
Not only that,
He knew his way around real estate
And had some friends on the Landmarks Commission.
Although a little illegal
He managed to get his building declared
A landmark due to the terra cotta work on the outside.
That way, the building could never be condemned
We had some wonderful times there…
Billy handled the news of AIDS
With a lot of balls…

He had an angle for a positive approach
Unfortunately, this time it didn't help
Larry and I didn't take the news well when
We heard...
Billy was already cracking jokes
About the AID'S plan for losing weight
We were numb...
When you know an important part of your
Life is about to end it leaves you
Devastated...and we were.

The first indication Billy had was
A dry wracking cough that wouldn't stop
And he was tired most of the time...
I think he knew but he couldn't
Bring himself around to admit it
To himself and certainly not us...
But finally, a purple lesion
The size of a half-dollar appeared
On his right cheek
And he could no longer hide it.

Billy was like all of us...
Vain and proud of his looks and body...
The weight just dropped off of him...
He became very reclusive, limiting
His contact with others to the phone,
But one day I got to him and talked
Him into leaving his house to come
Uptown for lunch...I even sent a

Limousine to bring him.
Just a caricature of his former self
But I loved him just as much and
After beating around the bush…
I said the word…AIDS!
When I did, it unleashed a torrent
Of pain, anger, and tears in Billy.
I felt so helpless…
He hated the idea of being sick.

We got rip-roaring drunk after lunch
And just spent the time hugging
Each other and crying…
We also laughed about the adventures
We shared over the years, and needing
That laughter, because we both knew…
But couldn't talk about it…dying
We also ripped every legend apart
We could think of…
Finally, while sitting in front
Of a roaring fire we let the afternoon
Unwind just communicating silently
Until Larry came home…

It's funny…
But as well as I know Larry
I've never seen him extremely emotional
So I fixed him a drink…
And we told Larry that Billy was dying.

You could have cut the silence with a knife...
Larry just stared into the fire,
Not saying a word
With the backdrop of Manhattan
And the cacophony of traffic below.

From the reflection of the fire's glow
I saw tears trailing their way
Down Larry's smooth cheeks.
He seemed to stare for a long while
Then jumped up and crashed his
Drink in the fire and went out on
The terrace as a loud sob escaped
His throat...
I didn't follow for a while
Because he needed to be alone...
I told Billy he can't die
Because although it's selfish
Larry and I love him too much

For him to leave us
Finally, I went out and saw that
Larry was shivering while leaning
Over the terrace just staring
At the magnificent city...
I quietly brought him a drink
And a sweater...
He mumbled thanks
And said...I don't want to cry...
When I cry it means there's sadness...

I hate sadness…
Life is for joy…
But I hurt for Billy…he's too damn good
Too big a part of us…our lives

Our hearts…he's there always.
Then Larry tossed his drink…
It shattered against the bricks
As the shards caught the light
Like a thousand diamonds
Flying through the air…
Larry looked up with his face contorted
With pain…
And screamed…Fuck God!

I had never heard him say Fuck God before.
I said Amen because both of those glasses were
Saint Louis Crystal.
For Billy's sake
He didn't have to suffer too much…
And when he was in the hospital
We saw that he had plenty of flowers,
Videos, and good food from his favorite
Restaurant…when he had an appetite…
I won't go into too much detail
About Billy's illness,
Because he would hate it…
There was a constant stream of friends
And clients…he was never alone.

Billy chose to die at home...and we were with him...
Billy died in my arms.

His family stayed away...
When he breathed his last breath...
I would not let go of his body...
Larry understood...but no one else did...
Finally, I had to face it and let go.
The sad thing was we couldn't find a
Funeral home that would take the body...
Then a friend of a friend knew a gay undertaker
Who graciously took care of the arrangements.
Billy will always be in my heart...

The family were total assholes...
They had his will thrown out of court...
To add insult to injury, I offered to
Buy the business but they sold it to
Billy's biggest competitor who Billy
Couldn't stand...
I tried to reason with his mother
Who said she wanted no reminders of
The way her son lived or died...

About three months after Billy was gone
This letter arrived from Billy's lawyer...

Dear Drew and Larry (My Two Princes),
Okay guys...chin up, don't cry for me, Concreta
'cause I had a ball. Honestly guys my life was rich

and exciting…full of texture and beautiful things, especially my two best friends. Let me say this to you two beautiful men, love each other now more than ever. Let those two hearts continue beating as one. Make love damnit, make beautiful things, and remember how full you made my life. Also, remember the wonderful times we had together, and hell, we all have to die…it's just that I would like to have stayed at the fair a little longer, that's all.

I will never know, but I hope my mother followed my wishes and had me cremated and the ashes thrown into the Hudson. If she didn't, please sweep the terrace at the bungalow, put the sweepings in a mayonnaise jar and sprinkle me in the Hudson at least symbolically. After all, I loved that…it was part of me. Just for a little drama, when you sprinkle me would you have a cassette player there and play Barbra Streisand singing "I Stayed Too Long at The Fair." I know I can depend on you guys to do this, and have as many of our friends there as you want.

I'm sure my family will fight the will…and I want you guys to have first option on buying the store and the building…but I know families can screw up wills, so to be safe, I left you two guys a pair of Louis XV chairs…and, no one knows about them. They're in the Manhattan Storage facility at Madison and 93rd. That's what the key in this letter is for. If you don't want them, they're worth a small fortune, and besides my family is into Levitz furniture anyway…God knows Louis XV wouldn't work in the Bronx. It's my way of saying thank you for all you gave to me, and all we shared over the years. The only regret I have is…is that I never found the right one, the right someone to hold me, and look in my eyes and say, I love you Billy…oh well. Promise me guys to please stay in love with each other and on my birthday you'll open a bottle of Cristal '79 and drink a toast to Billy Rutger, who like Auntie Mame thought life was a banquet and ate his fill.

I Love you,
Billy

Needless to say,
I couldn't get through his letter
The first time without crying,
'Cause there's a little piece
Of my heart that's gone forever.
So I put the letter away until
One night Larry came home and we
Got rip-roaring drunk and read the
Letter as we drank toast after toast
To Billy to end the grieving process
And after we read it, we sobbed until
We were dry as bones…

Having people like Billy in your life
Is what makes life worth living.
Larry and I pledged to stay in love
Forever…and the chairs look great
In our living room.

Through some foul-up of Billy's lawyer,
This letter arrived the following day.
I opened it before I realized it was
Addressed to Billy's mother.

Dear Mom,
I know you hated being called Mom, but I wanted to
do it one more time…'cause you were my mom. I had
to write this letter to you…it's important for you to
know who I was. I was your son…you gave birth to me.
I will apologize for not being the son you always wanted
and that's as far as I will go. I know you could never accept
the fact that I was gay, and it caused you great pain. Mom,
please understand, it wasn't your fault…it's no one's fault
and there's nothing to have fault about. I had a wonderful…
brilliant life. It was a beautiful adventure surrounded by
beautiful people (inside and out), and beautiful things. I
did everything I wanted to do except find the right
person to fall in love with. I don't regret much except
our not being close. I wanted to please you so badly
Mom, but I couldn't change to please you…change
what I am…was. Believe me, I'm not writing this to
hurt you…that's the farthest thing from my mind.

Mama, I'm tired and I need to rest. I hate dying and not being able to do a damn thing about it. I hope you understand a little more about your son. I know you tried to do the best you could, and so did I.

With Love,
From Your Child,
Billy

P.S. If you ever want to know more about me, call
My best friends, Drew and Larry at (212) 555-1974

We managed to find Billy's mother through Billy's lawyer and it was around ten days before we heard from her. She called and asked if she could meet with us and of course we invited her to the apartment.

We weren't quite expecting such a dowdy little woman as arrived. She looked as if she had the weight of the world on her shoulders. We gave her a drink asked her to sit then we spent the next five minutes in silence and then a torrent of words spewed forth.

She said, "I'm sure you read my son's letter. So, I would like to know more about him. I found out he was gay fifteen years ago. You see I was raised by very religious parents, and it's against everything his father and I believed in. Then I read his letter and went to my minister who told me he was also gay. I read the letter to him and my minister said, he'd wished he'd known my son. He sounded like the kind of young man he wished he'd had the opportunity to know and maybe love. So that's why I'm here. Please tell me about my son."

Larry motioned for me to talk as he couldn't. I said, "Mrs. Rutger, I'm sorry you missed out knowing Billy. He was kind, generous, fair, maybe twenty more adjectives I could use to describe him, but I don't want to cry. If you're here to relieve some guilt, don't. You missed an opportunity to know an incredible young man, who did nothing more than spread love, kindness and goodness wherever he went. And if you're so religious why the fuck can't you understand that if God loved your son, why couldn't you?

She looked at me with world weary eyes, then said, "After hearing about my son from you and other friends, and my minister, I wish I had. I'm not much of a talker, but I'll say this now. If I could have him back right now, I'd love that boy any way he was. But that won't happen and I'll just be a bitter old woman who will live the rest of her days in regret."

Well, we heard that she volunteers five days a week for God's Love We Deliver, a charity that brings meals to those with AIDS.

Yes...We're Guilty

Alright,
We finally got called on the carpet...
Larry and I were guilty of
Sticking our heads in the sand,
Even though we sent a grand each
For the cause...

Billy's death traumatized us both,
But we still hadn't gotten the message...
AIDS is alive and well in our friends...
It killed the best one we ever had...
We still chose to ignore it
Other than to acknowledge
That it existed and killed Billy Rutger.

We immediately went to be tested...
The results were negative...
Thank you, Jesus...
And again
We just sort of pretended
It never came to the upper
West Side...

So we go to our friend Irving's
For a dinner party
And seated next to me
Was a gay rights advocate

From California
Strictly from hostile city...

Larry was lucky,
He was seated next to Jewel Lark
The hottest new star on Broadway,
And she kept him in stitches
All through dinner.
The gay rights advocate
Bart Nash,
Who was out for blood,
After the first course of
Mussel Soup...chilled and
Straight from the Glorious Food
Cookbook, only with some tarragon added,
Why can't faggots leave the spice rack alone?
Mr. Nash looked straight at me
And in an icy voice said...
How much money have you given
To the fight against AIDS?

I ignored him and had another
Glass of champagne (It wasn't Cristal)

He wouldn't let up and asked me again.
So, in a very soft whisper,
I replied it was none of his business...
He pretended he was offended
And in a louder voice he said...
Am I to understand you don't support

The fight against AIDS?
Of course, now everyone was looking at us.
I said, that's not what I said,
But damnit he had me on the defensive…
Then I said, let's drop it…
One thing I will do, is fight when
I have my back up against the wall
And I was about to lay into this guy…
Our host was bright enough to
Change the subject…
And I was willing to forget about it…
But no…
This asshole…
Starts harping about the disease…
How important the fight is
And we should all do as much as we can!

The other guests are becoming a little
Embarrassed for the host…
Then the guy turns to me again…
Very slowly he says again

Am I to understand you don't support
The fight against AIDS?
Dead silence in the room…
I looked at him for a moment
And simply said,
That's not what I said…
What I said when you so rudely asked me
How much money I gave to the cause

Was that it was none of your business…
Then I said, now watch my lips you
Asshole…and hear me out…
It's none of your fucking business
How much money I give to any cause…

He was shocked to say the least,
But I wasn't finished.
Then I said
How much money have you and your effete friends
In the Land of La given to Broadway Cares or
The Actors fund?
We've lost a lot of actors, singers, and dancers
Who appear in Broadway shows that
Become movies that make a lot of you
People rich in Hollywood.

Everyone was relieved especially
When Bart jumped up, excused himself,
And left in a huff…
We all applauded…
Of course, he won…
The rest of the evening's conversation
Was about AIDS…
No one, unless they can get in my skin
Knows the deep loss I suffered when Billy died…
His memory will be with me always…
And the sad thing about his death,
Is that he didn't know what he was fighting.

On the walk home I told Larry
I was sorry for being such an ass,
And he assured me he would have done
The same thing.
I also suggested we phone Billy's doctor
The next day and see how we could
Best be of help.
I arranged to meet Dr. Alex Steinberg
For lunch the next day…
I liked the man immediately…
And wonder upon wonder,
It turned out he's gay…
He's seen a couple of my plays,
And reads my magazine articles…

Then we got down to business,
And a glass of wine at Mortimer's,
The worst place I could pick
As we both knew half the room.
We started talking about Billy
And before you knew it,
Little tears were escaping from
My eyes and finding their way down my cheeks…
But I did manage to keep control
Of myself…

Other than what I read,
And firsthand experience with Billy,
I had no idea how serious the
Disease was…

Alex explained that the biggest problem
Was for patients to find money for
The horribly expensive drugs they
Had to take to stay alive...

Believe me I was shaken
And resolved to do all I could...
I met Larry for tea
And on the way home
We decided we would each establish funds
To buy AZT for two patients
Every month until a cure was found...

And since we both agreed,
And it was Larry's idea...
We donated the money anonymously
And decided not to take it as
A tax write-off.
So...
That's what we do now,
Plus we support every fund-raiser
That comes our way,
And I am planning a series of articles
On young men with the disease...
Thank God we're healthy and can help...
Thank you, Bart Nash for opening our eyes!

Just Below the Surface

I'm a little nervous…

Okay paranoid…

Now Larry tells me everything's okay…

But I'm intuitive

And I know that man

Like I know my own face

And something's just not kosher…

Larry's been moody

Not grumpy…

Maybe the word is distant

That's it…distant

I see it in his eyes

And our lovemaking lately has

Been intense

With a touch of desperation in it.

Larry's been clinging

And without being a shrew

I ask him if all is okay

With us and the world…

He says of course!

Now I' know I'm not making this up

There's just something a little off

He seems preoccupied

As if he's in deep thought

With a touch of sadness just below

The surface.

I can't force him to reveal
What's in the recesses of
His mind and thoughts…
Hell, we're all entitled to privacy
But if there's something wrong here
Then all I want is fair warning
And a chance to make it all right.

I've been trying to learn
A little about the stock market
So, I can discuss it intelligently
And according to all I read,
The stock market is having
Record days…so I doubt it's
His job or career area…

He could be having trouble with
His family and some old friends.
We never discuss the parents or
His Wall Street life…
His parents have never and will never
Accept that their son is a homosexual
He's not dead in their minds…
He's just away for awhile.

Larry's father is a very powerful
Man in the financial community
And I'm surprised he hasn't
Pressured Larry into leaving me
And going straight…

When I'm in this space
Is the time I really miss
Billy Rutger…
Damn I miss him…
Used to be I would call him
And he would have me set straight
In no time at all…
Anyway…
I haven't talked about holidays
For this very reason.

On Thanksgiving and Christmas
I have to share him with the
Family…
The whole clan is polite…
They never bring "it" up
And I don't exist…period.
He goes to the family enclave
In Westchester County…
Stays a perfunctory amount of time
And then…thank God
He comes home.
I can't blame him…
He's had this preppy bullshit
Drummed into him since he was two.
He's not the same man when he
Comes home.
It seems his father takes him
Into the study for a Cognac
And a little "man to man" talk.

It's two to three days of quiet recovery
And then he's back to normal.

That's my analysis of the situation,
And as long as Larry says
Everything is all right
I have no defense.
Maybe we've also grown comfortable
And a little of the spark is gone…
God, I hope not…
Although the passion certainly
Isn't any cooler…
No as a matter of fact that
Just gets better and better.
Also, I'm flying off to California
And I'm going to miss him like crazy…
Just Can't Help Loving…

Once the Passion Goes

My biggest fear…and it is larger than life
Is that I will grow old and boring
No one will want me
I won't be stimulating, or,
Exciting, or,
Able to speak witty gems of wisdom
Or God forbid
Not be able to attract anyone…
Of course, I'm being silly
I notice I have been silly a lot
Since you've been hanging around
Why is that?
It is your power
Your ability
To make me feel like a kid
Is it the child you bring out in me?
I don't know
And I'm not sure I want to.

I look at you standing in front of the fire
Dressed in those faded blue cords
And cardigan sweater
And I see the man I want to grow old with.
I didn't think it would be a lover
I thought I would grow old with a friend
Probably Billy…
Yes, once all the lovers had left

And the houses and the "things" were gone
And I had seen and done it all
And would be happy in the company of a friend
Mainly because the friend would know
All about me and still love me
Whereas a lover would probably judge…
Things change
And so has my idea about growing old.
When I see you in front of the fireplace
I realize it's you, and I want to be with you always
If you're there
Then hopefully the passion will stay…
I really believe you die when your passion
Is gone…
And passion can be for simple things
Such as a bird singing outside your window
Or for your art and creativity
Or people walking by
Or children and dogs
Anything as long as it's something
That makes you want to make the bed
A reason to get up…
I will always make the bed for you,
Unless you're still in it.

The Night Before Leaving for the Coast

Drinks at the Oak Bar…
Looking out on the sidewalks and the park
Through the flicker of golden candlelight
Playing on our faces
That barely matches the sparkle in our eyes.
A quiet wistful walk over to Petrossian
To sit on a mink-covered banquet
And share some Beluga and Cristal '79
Occasionally there's an acidic stare from
Some asshole who wants to deny us our right to love
As we return the stare with our best fuck you smiles.
It just so happens that we're coming up
On our third…hard to believe
I notice we're a little quiet tonight…
Very unusual for us,
But I figure we're just reflecting…
Larry seems troubled…
I ask…
He says no…
I say, you're sure…?
He says yeah…
Just a little tired…
I get off it…

As we do on special occasions,
We indulge in a restaurant orgy…

Hitting several of our favorites,
Here on Concreta,
And embark on an adventurous
Progressive dinner.
Because we go out so much,
Restaurants are our second home…
After Petrossian,
It's Patsy's for pasta
It's almost a dive
But the food is to die for…
For the main course
We cab it to Café Des Artistes.
The atmosphere…
So romantic…
Larry has saddle of lamb,
And I have loin of veal with Chanterelles…
Oh Hell yes,
Harlequin Souffles with banana fudge sauce
And whipped cream
We linger over coffee and Grand Marnier.
Since we're both too full to move,
We take a hansom cab back to the apartment
For exquisite love making…
California…here I COME!

Spanish Tiles and Palm Trees

I should feel grateful,
Grateful that this studio wants to pay me
Bags of money to write classy television as they say…
I think the producer said he likes my class
Unfortunately, the leading lady's class is all third

I am ensconced in a two bedroom ultra-modern
Also done-to-death perched on a bluff
Overlooking forever, beach house
Which I should be grateful for
But I'm not because you're not here

Things are slow here
Days pass slowly
It is too beautiful here
It is difficult to feel
Because you see only beauty
Whereas in the "Apple"
You see the dirt and all that's wrong

I can't wait to get back to you
Where my heart and thoughts lie
Where the core of my being resides
Every time a wave crashes
I think about summers we've spent
On Martha's Vineyard
At Davis Park on Fire Island
The oceans are different

Just as the make-up of two lovers
Are different
Dammit, I miss you
I miss our life together
I could be happy here
If you were here
But you're not.

Malibu is sort of stark
Stark is a good word
It's foreboding
I thought I saw Karloff at the window
And then I thought if he was there
You would probably save me...right?

One luxury though is time
I use it well,
I laid on the beach yesterday for a couple of hours
I'm getting a little golden
Not tan, golden with a glow
While reflecting on the beach...nice title, huh?
By the way, I haven't written shit,
Can't get inspired
What I am inspired about,
Is that we have been together three years.
Three years is an amazing amount of time!
Time for anything
But especially for two hearts
To be intertwined
Wrapped around each other tightly.

And odds have it
That men in relationships don't last
Usually not more than a year
Two at the most
Wait until I get home.

If you were here
Maybe you could help me write this script
I have no ideas
I just want to lie on the sand
And think about you
About us
Maybe on a desert island
In a wonderful little bungalow
With a Spanish tile roof
And one big palm tree in the yard.

And Now, A Word From The West Coast

I haven't a clue why people live here.
Other than the weather
And the physical beauty of the place.
The best way to describe Los Angeles,
Is that it's a basic bungalow with
Wonderful acreage that a decorator
Put together in the eclectic style,
And the damn thing works.

It's certainly not the architecture...
There's no Chrysler Building,
No Dakota,
No Plaza Hotel,
But there is Harper House,
And the Colonial House,
And the Chateau Marmont,
And Bel-Air.

The West Coast is also lacking
Something else very important...
One gorgeous man with green eyes
And chestnut hair.

The studio has me working on a completely
Different project than what we started.
Shooting starts in three weeks,

And they want me to repair the dialogue.
They like my plays.
I like their money…
It's an even match.

There's also talk about a new dramatic series,
And I would I have to be here for 30 weeks a year.
Would you consider living in paradise
For half the year?
I'm going to ask when I get back.

The studio would lease a house to my liking,
Have the prop department decorate it,
And they would even give me associate
Producer status on the episodes if I'll
Consider it…just think about it.

The studio is very convincing.
Bernie Klein the new studio head had
A studio V.P. in a limo take me to see
A property the studio owns.

It's off Benedict Canyon Drive at the top
Of a knoll off Deep Canyon Dr.
It's at the end of a charming winding
Country Road…fifteen minutes from
Rodeo Drive and the rest of civilization.
I wasn't even going to go,
But they upped the money a $1,000 a week.

So I go see this house,
And it's love at first sight.
Not only that,
Bernie knows "my story" as he
Politely says.
If I come out to the West Coast,
He'll get you a senior V.P.
Job with a top brokerage firm in town
That invests the studio's portfolio.

The only thing is I'm not sure about,
Is the pace here.
There's no energy, other than
Lethargy.
Everybody is sort of pretty.

I'll have to go to a friggin' gym.
You wouldn't have to yet.
Nobody walks here,
That's why they're all in gyms…

I told Bernie I would have to think
About everything.
So Bernie says go back to New York
Think it over and call him.
In the meantime,
He wants me to write from the studio's
New York office 'cause they have a
Computer…
Everyday I can transmit the script
By laser…ain't that a kick?

By the time I'm on the plane
I know the answer.
I'm not even going to put it to a question.
I would rather be in New York.
It's my home, my roots…
And if you ever leave me,
Bloomingdale's is there.

I can't wait to see you…

That Day

I felt the quietness...
How much like you...
To leave everything so immaculate...
Your timing, so perfect...
Me on a trip to the West Coast
And you obviously with a list of things to do...
Every drawer relined...
The closets re-painted...
A stack of new books
For me to read...
To kill time...
Thought it all out didn't you?
A dozen new films for the VCR...
And the refrigerator stocked with my favorites...
Joseph Drouhin Puligny Montrachet '83...
Pecan chicken and new potato salad
From Word of Mouth
Caembazola from Zabars...
Hell, the windows were even cleaned...
How nice, how thoughtful...
Who could ask for a better homecoming...?
It was just so damn quiet
Just one small detail missing from
This *Metropolitan Home Magazine* picture...
YOU!
On the bed a sealed note written on your
Best monogramed Smythson stationary

Such an elegant touch
I will never forget those words
After I opened it
After I read it
And re-read it
And digested it
And re-read it
And screamed like a wounded animal

Dear Drew,

I know you won't understand and will have every reason in the world to hate me, but please don't. I can't explain now, but I have to break this off before I break up. I can't explain why, I just need to leave…be alone, maybe for a short while, maybe forever. I don't know for now, but I need the time to find out who I am… what I want. This is not the coward's way out, but if I had done this in person I might not have been able to. I trust you'll respect my wishes. It was beautiful for so long, wasn't it?

Love,
Larry

It was beautiful, Love Larry…
That's the part I couldn't believe.
How the hell can you say that…
You don't do that to someone you love
Please God,

Help me make it through the time I will need…
That was my first thought
And then I felt calm…
That I would be alright.

I'm very fortunate,
And I thank God that I can use the written word…
I will be able to work my way out of this…
This pain…
This Goddamn, horrible insidious pain
That's ripping my fucking guts
Right out of my body…
Oh, I'm sure
It will probably not happen in one day…

My regret is that you're not inside of me
So that you can experience this pain
To know how I really feel.
You couldn't have been more cruel…
Without meaning to be.
I know you…
You couldn't hurt anyone…
Not me…
If I could scream on paper I would

This could be a mistake.
That's it…it's a mistake…
Okay, a joke
The fun's over
Come on out

Ollie Ollie oxen free . . .

Come on out...

You might find out tomorrow

You were wrong

It was a mistake

You were nuts for a day

This stock market shit-canned

You weren't yourself...

I know how hard you brokers work.

It's what I'm hoping for.

But...

Down inside I feel a chill

This might just be permanent

You were too careful

As if you've been planning this

I can even guess how you feel...

But we love each other damnit...

Or so I thought...

People who love don't do this to each other...

They sit down and have civilized talks

They explain it is not working

Agree to a trial separation

Try to make it work

Please...

I won't beg

Let me wake up and know it's a bad dream

Maybe from indigestion like Scrooge thought

When he saw the ghost

My arm is already bruised from pinching.
Does Hallmark make a card for this?
Dear Man,
Thank you for killing me!

God damn if we could,
Could have just gotten through the winter
Manhattan is so damn cold in February
I'll have a new day to mark in my date book.
February 17…
I will always remember that day
A Tuesday…that day.

Many Things Will Change

More than anything else

I never wanted anything

At anytime

In this or any other life

Any season

Any second

Any day, week, month, or year

Did I ever want anything

As much as I wanted you...

How dare you affect me this way

What an obsession you have become

My hobby,

My purpose,

Which is why you probably left me

God dammit!

I was so careful

I let you be the strong one

And I had one hell of a time

Giving up my power

Letting you pick the film

Choose the restaurant...

I hate Thai food

I loathe art films

Although

If I had to do it once again

I would eat every strange thing,

And smile through every

Indian, French, Russian, Turkish and Israeli film we saw
I would even stay awake through them
If only…
If only…
If there was the remotest chance…
Damn this isn't easy
I have removed every trace of you
Except one!
Your Goddam cologne
Which permeates every crevice
Every nook and cranny of this
Oh so drop-dead decorated-to-death tomb.
Every time I smell Atkinson's Royal Briar
I want to scream
I almost cry
Because I think of the first night you stayed over
You asked if you could shave
Because your beard is so thick
And you broke the valve on the lather can
You were so embarrassed
As you lost your well-constructed composure
I tried not to laugh at you with shaving cream dripping
And then I lost it and so did you
Jesus Christ almighty
I don't know how much more of this I can take.
My agent called
My play, "Nights End" will be revived.

I'll never forget your going to the reading…
And when the hero was dying

And the heroine told him how much she loved him
Out of the corner of my eye
I saw your reaction.
You were weeping
Ever so softly
Then you sort of clutched your heart
And you were endeared to me through the ages.
I have been told to let go of you
Whatever the hell that means…
I can't…
I just can't…
I wish I could.

I will have this apartment repainted
Have all the rugs, carpets, upholstery, and drapes cleaned
That will do it for the cologne.
I wish I could erase you like a tape
I have analyzed all of this
Dissected my feelings
I have placed myself on an exhaustive schedule
Trying to drive you from my silly brain
Nothing works.
And I know
That with each day
Many things will change
But more than anything else.
I still love you so.
And I wish I didn't…

River, Hell... I Damn Near Cried an Ocean

I was doing just fine and dandy...
My particular way of getting through the day
And I might add over you,
Was to get up in the morning,
Bolt for the park
And jog 'til near exhaustion
Making sure I end up on the East Side
So I can slowly walk back
To the West Side...
The scene of the crime...
And the walk helps me kill time...
Which I have plenty of lately...
On arrival back in the apartment
I immediately turn on the stereo
Drop in a cassette of "I Will Survive"
Which I've recorded five times in a row.
And I play that damn tape
Over and over again
Until I bullshit myself into relief
So I can get on with my day...
So I hate you a little less...
You would be so proud of me
I've been so strong...
Blaming no one
Getting through nicely
With the help of some midnight phone calls

To irate friends
Who are sick of me talking about you!
I haven't blamed you
For piercing my heart
Or blamed me for letting you…
I have behaved wonderfully
Called on all my strength
All the esoteric jargon, advice
And spiritual bullshit
One can possibly muster,
Plus an inner-well of fortitude
I just never knew existed.
I don't really hate you…
I want to hate you…
So I pretend I hate you
And then I listen to
Rupert Holmes singing "I Don't Need You"
Except I do and admit it.
I'm not ready to analyze why
I'm still too raw
And I can't dare let myself…
Let myself wonder if you'll come back
That maybe this is a mistake.
Sarah won't put me through at your office,
My name is not Nancy Sinatra…
Who thinks Frank is coming back…
I have accepted that as Gospel…
And another thing…
You needn't worry about me
Setting traps for you just in case…

Just in case you should have to drop by
For any reason that is...
No, I'm clever and you pack well.
You didn't leave one damn thing behind...
Except a trace of your cologne in everything
And...a heart that looks like hamburger.

For my health
I have to hold all this in...
Here's why...
Because if I ever let go of my emotions
I don't know what I would do...
How I would react...
I have managed to stay fairly sane...
Believing that this is part of life,
And that I am not the only person
This has ever happened to
Nor will I be the last...
You see Larry, I am very controlled...
You are gone...dead... dissipated into thin air.
But you're not, no you're...

I have a clear path to walk down.
And I know if I follow this advice
I will be alright.
There are always factors one has no control over,
For instance,
I went to the dry cleaners today
To put some fall things into storage,
And to take some heavy sweaters out...

And gee

Wouldn't you know it…

You just weren't as careful as you thought.

I get home with the package…

Tear off the plastic and paper…

You know I hate all that tissue stuck up the arms

Of jackets and sweaters,

And I'll be a son-of-a-bitch!

Hiding there between two of my sweaters,

Was that beautiful silk and cotton cardigan

I gave you for your birthday…

You just can't imagine how I felt…

Just in the nick of time

I looked at my watch

Only to find out I was late for my lunch date

So I knew I didn't have the time to fall apart

And put my emotions on hold…

Damn I was proud of myself…

Off to lunch at Café Des Artistes…

Well, I had to go there sometime…without you

Just because it was our favorite place

Doesn't mean I will give it up…

My publisher and I had our meeting…

The food was fabulous as always

And I had forgotten about that damn sweater…

In fact, from the two martinis I had at lunch

I had a nice warm glow

And looked forward to the walk back
Seeing as how it was such a brisk day.

I'll be damned...
The minute I walk outside
Guess who goes by in a chauffeured car?
I would know your face in a cave...
I suppose the word should be daze...
'Cause that's what I was in
I just stood there for a minute
And I don't even remember
When I started walking...
But I lost it about 71st Street.
I didn't sob,
There were just a couple of small tears
Coming out of each eye...
Slowly sliding down my cheeks...
I blamed it on the breeze from the Hudson blowing in my eyes...

You would have been so damn proud of me...
I made it through the lobby
To the elevator
And before I could get to the apartment
I met everyone I had ever known in that God forsaken building...
But I finally got inside
And bolted the door
Lit a fire
Turned up the music
Went into the bedroom

Closed off the drop-dead view
Fell on the bed...
And I let it out in great torrents of pain...

It wouldn't stop
And my body shook from the sobs...
They literally made me think I would lose my breath
But I couldn't stop...
So I got up from the bed...
Tried to wash my face
Without looking in the mirror...
And then I remembered that God damn sweater.

And I took it and ripped the fucking thing
To pieces
While pretending it was you...
Then I threw it in the fireplace...
And said your eulogy...
At that moment I didn't know I could hate
Hate anyone so much...
But I didn't really hate you
I hate what the loss of your love has done to me
I hate the way I feel.
I had a brief reprieve
But I couldn't focus on what my next move would be.
This apartment has never been so lonely
If there was just a pill
Or a drink
Anything I could take to feel better...
I would

But there isn't
And time doesn't come in a bottle or pill form...
I don't give a fuck what the songs say...
Experience has taught me
Time is the only tested answer and cure...
And I have so much of that.
I really thought the crying was over
Until I went to the kitchen...
And as I looked up on the fridge door
I realized the calendar was still there
With some dates for future evenings with friends...
And I lost it again!
I just stood there and sobbed...
I'm not sure when I stopped,
I just know it was dark.
Although I felt like I had cried an ocean
Over you
Instead of a river like the song says,
At least I felt some relief...
Relief from this pain
This never ending pain
Which is only a loss...
A loss of love.

Is It Door Number...

Okay, I made all the choices,
I have no one to blame,
And I don't blame myself,
For what…loving?

I don't even have guilt,
For a Jewish boy that's something…
Why should I?
I'm at my best when I'm in love,
And I hope I love again,

Before Larry,
There was Robert,
That was four years,
And believe me,
When he went away I thought I'd die,
But I didn't, and when I didn't,
I knew there was much more,

It boils down to once again,
Making a choice,
I could have chosen to be alone,
And I am damn good at being alone,
I'm damn good company,
Even on those Goddamn snowy days,
And I was after Robert,

It took six months to get over that pain,
And pain is only the loss of something,
Unfortunately,
The pain of human withdrawal is the worst,
There is no remedy that works quickly,
Oh you can use food,
Or drugs,
Or compulsive sex,
Or booze,
Or shopping,

Then you find out that the above
Are only quick fix-its
And run the risk,
Of spending the rest of your life,
In a twelve-step program,

So, there's door number 1: Not getting involved ever again.

I'm not ready to talk about "after Larry,"
I haven't accepted that yet,
This is about after love period.
So after Robert, I threw myself into work,
Jumped out of bed, showered,
And hit the typewriter six non-stop hours a day,
Created what I thought was my best work,
And refused to think of anything that happened…
I completely stayed in a fog,
And any moment that his face popped in my head,
I changed the channel,

I would think of horrible food combinations,
Like oysters and hot fudge with coffee ice cream,
Shad Roe with mint jelly and peanut butter

So, there's door number 2: Becoming a workaholic to forget.

The second choice after losing love,
Is like overcoming the fear of falling off a horse,
Getting right back up while the pain is fresh,
(I like the sound of that, fresh pain)
That's right charging right back out there,
Taking that old heart and throwing it out there,
Not giving a damn where it landed,
I just knew I had to try again,
Life's too short not to have the best,
Live for feelings…good feelings about myself,
Especially when I'm entwined under the sheets,
With a gorgeous man,

So, there's door number 3: Getting involved again.

These choices were the past,
I'm not sure what the future will hold,
Although I've loved other men,
I've never loved like I loved you,
Each person has their one great love,
And you were it Larry!
So for now,
I can get through this drunk,
Or

Get to work and write the best damn play ever,
Or
Get back to window with my binoculars,

So,
Is it door:
Number one:
Number two:
Or
Door number three?

Who the fuck am I kidding?
There's only one door and that's the one that
Leads me back to you.

Comparing Him to You

What an unfair thing to do to someone…
The first date after the break-up…
Jesus Christ couldn't get through this test!
He does a hundred things that you do
Except when you do them it's all right
When he does them I want to scream!

You look at his features
He has lines in his face from age
Yours were laugh and character lines
This man, poor bastard, has no character
He's not funny
He's boring, and he's trying his best.

I notice his shirt is not as perfectly pressed as yours
His jacket has a thread hanging from it
I'm looking at the material
Just to see if there is any polyester
You could have dressed in double knit
I wouldn't have cared,
And this man does have taste
But he's not you.

Of course the restaurant he picked was dreadful
The Manhattan Ocean Club
The white fish was tough
The salad was wilted

The bread was stale
The wine was too young
The table was wrong
The waiter was rude
The asparagus was soggy
The hollandaise had broken
The lighting was harsh

His jokes weren't funny
I could care less about his fucking career
What was he, a lawyer, or something
Won some prestigious award
Everyone knew him
Called him sir and treated him with respect
I think he has the beginnings of a blemish
His perfect white teeth are probably
The result of the attention of six dentists.

And then the recital at Carnegie Hall
Please spare me the cello music
That old barn is drafty
It creaks when you walk
The red velvet seats are getting worn.
The audience takes themselves too seriously

And if that wasn't enough
It was to the Beekman Tower for drinks
And of course the fucking fog rolled in
Which obstructed our view
And then I had to gaze into his cloudy

Blue eyes, which were gray in the light
And he smoked, but didn't
When he found out I didn't
Such a gentleman.

And wouldn't you know it,
He's a Sondheim freak
And not only that
He likes Rupert Holmes
I'll kiss your ass if he's not from
Central Casting
This jerk also likes
Vanessa's in the Village
And guess what else?
His favorite is Café des Artistes.

His next suggestion is going back to his place
I say why not
So off we go to a wonderful apartment
That fronts Gramercy Park
Huge Palladian windows
A fireplace
Original mahogany paneling
And to top it off
It's decorated eclectically
Which is our…I mean my favorite style

Now why am I staying for a drink?
The music is right
The night is perfect…a chill in the air

The fireplace is roaring
And there's a jacuzzi in the basement
With a fireplace
This is a movie set
He's lonely
His lover left him six months ago…I know that one
He's had a wonderful time
He likes my company
He thinks I'm attractive
He's seen my work
And even knows the motivation for some of the characters
Too good to be true
The Jacuzzi's too hot

Yes I would like to see the bedroom
He's putting his arms around me
I hate his cologne
He needs to shave
His mouth tastes like Scope
He's taking off his clothes
He's leading me to the bed
He has a fabulous body

Why am I not turned on?
He's nuzzling my ear
It usually drives me crazy
It's not tonight
He's gently kissing my shoulders
It's not working
He turns back the bed…

I just watch
And then he leads me to the bed
And I get in under the covers
He begins exquisite foreplay
I'm about half stimulated
I make him stop
He's not happy about it, but he does.
Like I said, a gentleman.

The next thing I know
I'm in a cab
Asking myself why I left.
What about this evening?
I love cello music
I adore the Manhattan Ocean Club
I contributed money to save Carnegie Hall.

He dressed with taste
He's handsome
He's also witty
He's refreshing
He's sexy
He's everything wonderful a man should be
Except one thing… he's not you!

Sub-Text-Aftermath-Drew

OH, FUCK, HE'S HERE,
    i knew it would happen,
    i just wish it hadn't been so damn public,
    damn it, you don't even look battered,
    sailing along like a sloop,
    not a line from weariness or pain,
    fresh tan…puerto rico or key west?

I WILL NOT TALK TO YOU SO DON'T COME OVER,
    you're still the best-looking man in the room,
    any room, anywhere
    and wouldn't you just know,
    you'd be wearing that paisley tie i gave you,
    our first Christmas together wasn't it?
    ain't that a bitch?

I HATE YOUR GODDAMN GUTS,
    i have never loved like this before,
    gave it all my man,
    would do it again,
    in a new york minute,
    wouldn't have to think twice,
    …i will never get over you,
    how the hell could you do this to me,
    i never was a victim and I'm not now,
    i can't fill the time,

all i do is see your face,
hear your fucking voice,
the pain never stops,
don't you even care at all?

I COULD CARE LESS

only about every minute,
of every hour, and day, and week,
the rest of my life,
it doesn't matter you walked out,
no explanation…nothing,
where's the bar,
i'll get so damn drunk,
been doing that a lot lately
i'll probably end up in aa!

BUT I HARDLY THINK ABOUT YOU EXCEPT EVERY OTHER FRIDAY,

i miss you so damn much,
i need you so badly,
and at night my body screams for you,
every cell, every nerve,
i miss sex with you,
the touching, the feeling, the kissing,
the licking, the sucking, the fucking,
the base needs fulfilled,
the sweat from two bodies spent in passion,
the rolling around on the bed,
the floor, the sofa,
the nights when we couldn't get enough,

the nights you said you'd be here forever,

i will never ever forgive you.

OH SHIT, YOU'VE SEEN ME,

please don't come over,

i'm not ready,

not enough time has passed,

give me a break please,

maybe you didn't see me,

SCOTCH AND SODA PLEASE,

thank you, why did I order this?

you drink scotch...I don't,

see how my concentration goes,

I hate the taste of this crap,

like drinking a fireplace,

goes down like fire,

but...nice warm glow,

mighty nice this scotch,

i wish the artist would make an appearance,

so I could go,

THANK GOD,

always there when I need you,

good...that ditzy blond with big tits got you,

uh huh...you stockbrokers...all alike,

she must think you're e.f. hutton,

the way she listens,

watch it bitch...not so close,

I've never hit a lady,
doesn't mean there won't be a first time,

NOW, ABOUT THIS ART,
most of it is major caca,
#9 is interesting.
love the cerise,
the artist probably cut off his cock for inspiration,
actually, it's damn good.
It would look good over our sofa…my sofa.
that's the problem with life right now…
having to change ours to mine and yours!

Sub-Text-Aftermath-Larry

I HAD A FEELING YOU WOULD BE HERE,
    i know how much you love this artist,
    i'm so glad there's so many people,
    i would hate a scene,
    you look great,
    how could i have done this to you?
    all the time i was in key west,
    i thought about you,
    i know i'm right though,
    i love you too much,
    i'm afraid,
    i need time,
    do you hate me?

PLEASE DON'T CATCH MY EYES LOOKING AT YOU,
    you look so wonderful,
    rested…kind…those eyes,
    they say so much…so much hidden,
    i love the black suit,
    double breasted always suited you,
    and that tie…
    i gave you that tie for your birthday,
    can i change?

YOU PROBABLY HATE MY GUTS,
    if you do i understand,
    it's hard to come to terms with

loving a man,
especially when your family groomed,
you to be straight all your life,
and the guilt from the church,
someday I hope you will understand,
i have to pray to get through almost,
every minute,
it's all I can do to keep from picking up
the phone and begging to come back,
i know one day we can get together and
talk about all this and laugh,
i can't give up my career, not even for you…
i've hurt my family so much,
do you hate me?

A Conversation Overheard (While in the Restroom of the Excel Art Gallery)

Man 1: "What do you think of the art?

Man 2: "What art? I'd call it crap!"

Man 1: "The crowd?"

Man 2: "Worse than the art."

Man 1: "Definitely here for the food and the drinks?"

Man 2: "Uh huh, check the shoes."

Man 1: "What?'

Man 2: "Check the shoes, it's a dead giveaway for funds."

Man 1: "It doesn't matter…the art's shit, the artist knows It…he doesn't worry…cause he's young, hung, and handsome…and Mikhail the gallery owner's crazy about him."

Man 2: "It's a good thing…although I liked #9."

Man 1: "You like anything nine, and that's common knowl edge."

Man 2: "Fuck you."

Man 1: "You'd love to."

Man 2: "I hear everyone in New York has…just kidding."

Man 1: "By the way, did you see Drew and Larry?"

Man 2: "I know…thought it would be a scene."

Man 1: "No, no, Larry's too much of a gentleman for that. So's Drew."

Man 2: "Personally I didn't think it would last three years."

Man 1: "You mean you hoped it wouldn't last three years, I

Man 1: "know you've always had a thing for Larry, and he wouldn't give you the time of day."

Man 2: "That's bullshit…we had a date."

Man 1: "The way I hear it, is that he finally agreed to go out with you so you would stop asking him, and then spent the whole evening discussing the merits of one of Drew's plays."

Man 2: "Okay, you're right. I did have such a crush on him. And he was crazy about Drew after one date. I don't see why. They're so different."

Man 1: "Drew's one hell of a guy. Talented writer,…so he ain't Tom Cruise."

Man 2: "What's strange though, is that no one knows why they split up…they're both so private and closed mouthed."

Man 1: "Something you've never achieved."

Man 2: "Up yours. The gossip is that Larry couldn't handle living a gay life, not after all those chances to marry the perfect little debutante and being such a preppy. His family is so old-line I think they built the Mayflower."

Man 1: "Yeah, even in these liberal times, old money doesn't spend gay anyway you look at it, raising heirs is the number one concern. Just where are you getting this information?"

Man 2: "The world is small. My hair cutter's sister's husband is Larry's father's driver. Stay with me. The driver sometimes keeps the intercom on between the front and back seat. He knows I know Drew, because I gave him a couple of tickets to one of Drew's plays."

Man 1: "No shit? By the way, you want some of what we came in here for?"

Man 2: "No way, I'm off that stuff, the old nose won't take it."

Man 1: "Anyway, back to what you were saying about Larry."

Man 2: "Right…my barber says that the driver tells him that on more than one occasion, Larry and his father have been arguing about his lifestyle which the father finds totally disgusting and it has to stop like poor Larry can flip a switch or something."

Man 1: "Larry doesn't put up with this shit does he?"

Man 2: "I'm getting to it…you see even though he's the top producer at the firm, the old man has some ties there, plus a hefty portfolio, and he tells Larry he will pull it and see that he doesn't work anywhere in New York ever again."

Man 1: "The old son-of-a bitch sounds ruthless to me."

Man 2: "You ain't heard nothing yet. Larry tells him to do whatever he wants to do, because he will live his life as he damn well pleases and that includes being with Drew."

Man 1: "That doesn't explain why they broke up!"

Man 2: He takes a sniff of coke. "I said give me time and I'll tell you everything. The old man tells Larry to think it over for a week and to get back to him like it's a business deal. So Larry tells his father, he's willing to risk his career to be with Drew. This infuriates the old man to no end and he plays the trump card. He tells Larry that he either ends this or he will see to it that Drew is exposed for what he is and will see him ruined.

Man 1: "I'll take a hit of that coke now." He snorts it. "So, Dad plays rough!"

About Being Loved…! 171

Man 2: "Uh huh. It gets worse. The old man has bought Drew's publishing company, will have him canned at the magazine, and knows the head of the theatrical union, and he'll make sure the unions never work one of his plays."

Man 1: "Shit, this would make a great movie, too bad there's no part for Bette Davis."

Man 2: "There's more. Do you remember Ruth Lawrence?"

Man 1: "You mean the big star from 25 years ago?"

Man 2: "Exactly. Larry's old man had a hot 'n heavy affair with her…helps her become a star. I think she starred in three shows and then you never heard from her. Well, he asked her to marry him, and she says no. So, he says either marry him or he would kill her career which he did. And you never heard from her again."

Man 1: "God that explains what happened to her. Every now and then at a party someone will bring up her name, but no one has an answer. Bet your ass that I'll be having a dinner party soon."

Man 2: "You'll keep your fucking mouth shut, because Drew and Larry have been through enough without your venom."

Man 1: "Who'd believe it anyway?"

Man 2: "Exactly. To finish, the old man says not only would he finish Drew's career, but if that wasn't enough, he'd have Drew finished too."

Man 1: "He'd do it …wouldn't he?"

Man 2: "In New York minute, and that's 32 seconds in Texas time. All he cares about is the family name and his money. Nothing else is important."

Man 1: "So I get the picture…to keep Drew from getting hurt, Larry quietly ends the love affair of his life while Drew's on the west coast."

Man 2: "It's hard to believe that one man could love another that much. But it's true. I would have blown my brains out."

Man 1: "What brains?"

Man 2: "Fuck you! And no, I wouldn't love to."

Man 1: "What would keep Larry and Drew from running off with each other?"

Man 2: "Here's another story. Do you remember a Martin Brentridge?"

Man 1: "The name sounds familiar."

Man 2: "Okay he was going to run for president in 1980. Well, Reagan was Lawrence Barton's boy. So Brentridge was considering running for President the same year. It seems that Brentridge was drugged and photographed with a male escort. Though not true, he didn't run."

Man 1: "I'm not sure I want to know this."

Man 2: "Larry's father would hunt them down. He would. Besides, with the success of some of his work, Drew being well known, both coasts accept being gay, but middle America still looks for our horns.

Man 1: "Maybe Larry's father will die soon."

Man 2: "He's only in his late fifties."

Man 1: "I was watching the two of them tonight…Larry is still in love with Drew as much as Drew is still in love with Larry."

Man 2: "I know…that's the kind of pain that kills you…and there is no cure except time."

About Being Loved…! 173

Man 1: "Maybe we're fortunate to be single."

Man 2: "I don't care what the risks are…I'd rather be in love anytime…that includes the pain, the heartache. It's the most incredible thing in the world…Love!

Dazed On The Throne

I suppose I sat there
At least another fifteen minutes.
Maybe because every part of my body was numb
—it was
Especially my brain
Then a tear from each eye
Made a little trail
Down each of my cheeks.
Then I came to my senses
And fumbled to get my pants up…
I raced like lightning
To see if there was the remotest chance
Just a chance that you might still be there.
You were gone…and
Listening to the two gossips in the can
Did not help anything
But at least it explained it
The mystery
The unanswered phone calls
The unanswered notes, and letter
The avoiding me… that was the most painful.

God,
Does this mean he still loves me?
It's been six months
Is there a chance?
What about the father?

Larry
I love you more than ever
Just seeing you tonight confirms
My feelings
They have not diminished
They've grown
Like the intensity of my work
Thank God for that work.
What am I saying?
He doesn't want me
He will listen to his father
But doesn't he know
His father can't hurt me.
This is 1988
It's going to be alright
I'm sure I saw flickers of fire in those eyes
I know the feelings are still there.
I will go by his building
I'll wait until he comes out
I have to tell him
I understand
After all,
I am willing to save my sanity
And my heart from closing.

Answering Machine Chronicles

I went directly from the gallery
To the closest phone I could find...
It was freezing on the street
But I was perspiring from nerves
Two people were ahead of me
Waiting for the phone...
I almost got macho and took it away...
I looked at my watch,
It was 9:34.

Next stop was Spring and Green Street
Where there was a phone
And damn...it was full of change...
Wouldn't take a thin dime,
It was 9:39.

I tried to get a cab...
Can you believe there never is one
When you desperately need it
I have no idea how to get on a bus
Or where they go...
So, I see a subway sign
And down into the bowels of the city...
Finally...a phone
It took my quarter
I dialed your number
And held my breath

Busy signal… damn
That could mean you're home
Or someone's calling your machine…

I dialed again…
555-4928
It was 9:46
One ring…
Two rings…
"Thank you for calling,
You have reached the residence
Of Lawrence Barton,
I cannot accept your call
At this time…
At the sound of the tone…
Please state your name,
Message, and time you called
And a number where you may be reached…
Thank you."

Talk about a tight-assed message…
Here's the subway…
Jesus, the subway really paints a picture
About how filthy the city has become.
An appropriate scent would be Urine number 1
It was 9:53.

I can't believe
I haven't spoken with you in six months
And it took all the power I had

I have respected your wishes
And not called you
And stopped writing
And stopped all efforts to see you...
Stopped waiting in front of your office to catch a glimpse...
Stopped waiting in front of your building...
All of you out there know the drill
Some would call it masochism...
Maybe it is...
I've already endured more pain
Than I thought was possible...
This has damn near destroyed me...
But damnit...
I'm entitled to an explanation,
And I want it...
I want you to look me in the eye
And tell me you don't love me...
If, and I say if you can tell me...
Then I will try and stop loving you...
Get on with my life...
Oh and don't worry about a divorce,
Our commitment ceremony wasn't legal...

I must really be insane
Traipsing all over this city
To ask a man to talk to me
Who may very well not wish to ever see me...
What am I saying?
I heard those two guys in the restroom...
They said you still love me

That you just surrendered to the wishes
Of your family and your father.
That's all I need to know…
That there's the slimmest chance
I can have you back…
Just a chance…
I'm not worried about your father…
FUCK HIM and what he's done to us…
I will always be able to work,
And trust me…
I could take pen and paper
And rap your old man about
A little insider information he might have
Not that he has…
But it would send the Feds crawling
Up his ass…just to see how he likes it…
No, not in 1988 will I be afraid
Of a threat to my career…
Besides, between the two of us
We don't ever have to work again…
It was 10:02

I love the Graybar Building on Lexington…
But not so much tonight…
I thought the subway ride to 14th Street
Would never end…
And then the cross-town shuttle
And then the number 6 Uptown
It was 10:14

I thought the train would never get to E. 68th St.
Hunter's College was quiet as a tomb
And my heart was pounding
Like a jack hammer
By the time I reached the street
It was 10:19

I can't believe there are all these phones
And all the people using the damn things...
Who the hell are they talking to at 10:21?

I have to calm myself...
I'm almost there
I know it will all be fine
Everything will be forgiven...
He'll beg me to forgive him
And I will...
The past will not be discussed
Unless he brings it up
We'll pick up where we left off...
Where is the fucking phone...?
There it is...
It was 10:22

I damn near broke my finger
Dialing the number...
It's busy, he's home...
I'm running...
Here's your building...
Stop beating so hard my heart...

Yes, Mr. Doorman,
Please announce me to Mr. Barton...
Yes...in 1426...
Just say Drew is in the lobby,
And would like to see him...
At first I thought the doorman had made a mistake...
He said Mr. Barton...doesn't want you to come up...
He will come down...
Please wait in the lobby...
It was the longest fucking five minutes
I have ever waited for anything...
He appeared and didn't say a word...
Just motioned me to follow him...
Damn, he won't let me look in his eyes...

Once on the street
He began walking swiftly
When we reached Lexington and 72nd,
He turned and stared at me...
It was 10:31
Then without any emotion he said,
Why are you here?
Don't you understand...it's over...
I have no feelings for you...
I have a new life...
Let's try to be civilized about all of this...
I was afraid this would happen when
I saw you tonight...
That's why I didn't speak to you
Or come over...

It's been six months,
So let's leave it the way it's been…
This way, it will remain pleasant.

I just smiled and stared back and said…
I know what you're doing.
You're trying to protect
Me and my career from your father…
I know the whole story…
I love you even more than ever…
We can have our old life back…
You and me…the two of us…
We do not have to be lonely any longer…

To which he replied…
I don't know where you get your information…
But you're wrong…
Let me be clear, it is over…
A stage I was going through…
I'm not gay,
I thought I was
But I'm not.
I don't want to be part of your perversion…
Or anything that goes with it…
Do you understand?
I have done my best in letting you down…
Easily I might add.
Now don't make me be harsh or cruel…
Being gay, or a fag, or a queer
Does not work for me…

Now leave me the hell alone...
A...L...O...N...E...do you understand?

I shook my head yes...
As I watched the shape
Of his gorgeous ass as he walked away
And there was no careless wave of his hand
For all my trouble...

Well by God!
This man isn't going to cry
Over that man...ever again!
I hailed a cab...
What I did not know...
Was that while I was entombed in my cab...
Taking the long ride back to the westside
Feeling a large degree of numbness,
Or maybe shock, or maybe not anything,
Lawrence J. Barton III was in his apartment
Doubled over in the fetal position sobbing and thrashing
On the floor
Realizing his huge loss as only someone
Who has loved can...

Something You'll Never Know

I have told you so many things.
How I feel,
How you've made me feel,
The way you've touched me,
The way I've touched you.
You see,
This is the way this Goddamn pain will leave.
If I keep puking words out of my brain
Until there's nothing left to say or feel
About you.

Damn you!
You made my fantasy come true.
Great feat...turned fantasy into reality!
My other lovers were wonderful,
Or what I thought were lovers.
But then you walked in...
No, you exploded right into my life.
I still can't explain the power you
Unleashed within me.
Made everything just real damn fine.
Made it okay for me to be me,
Okay to be me in love.
Half-crazed, half-aware,
Aware of everything and motion around me.
I no longer had to hide my heart,

Because I became part of something beautiful.
And why does it cause so much pain?

I want to scream so loudly
That this fucking paper would shred
So that all these letters would fall off.
I'm so afraid.
I'm afraid I won't ever love again.
I can't bullshit myself.
I need to be loved.
And I was…loved, loved
Better than anyone has the right
To be loved.
And Goddamit,
You took that away from me.
You took the core of my soul away.
I can't even hate you for it.
So, if I tell you these things to your face,
It's still something you'll never know,
Because you're not me,
You're not inside me,
Except you are…
And if I can't have you, completely,
Then you have to leave me completely!
And here we are again…back to time.

Over the Rainbow

The place I found myself in after
Hearing that from Larry
Was not over the rainbow.
I suppose I had toughened
And in my heart, I was prepared for the worst
Which it was.
Men like Larry don't grow on trees,
Or live in them for that matter.
Hell, it hurts,
The finality
The bluntness,
And how your head can run away
With all sorts of thoughts,
And it begins to destroy your confidence,

The Goddamn pain
Fills every crevice of your being
Just like his fucking cologne filled the apartment
A constant reminder.
And then come the clichés,
About time and healings,
And tomorrows and how all will
Be just fine and dandy.
Bullshit!
It takes years to get over a love affair.
And just because they've had enough,
Collect their marbles and decide

Not to play anymore,
Does not mean it's fine.
They may have the marbles damnit,
But my broken-down old heart
Was the playing board.
I want to be in love,
I deserve to be in love,
And world…I need to be in love
Because I am really alive then.

After our encounter on the sidewalk
I was absolutely numb.
I don't know what I expected,
But it sure as hell wasn't
Screaming!
But if I know anything,
I know that man…
He's in me and I'm in him…
Unfortunately, so is a lot of guilt
From his family.
Maybe I should have done the same thing…
Maybe not.
But I wrote him one last letter,
So here it is…

Dear Larry,
I don't need to tell you that I love you, you know that. I also know you love me. Go ahead and deny it; to me, to the world, to yourself. But you do. And you know how I know? Last night the whole time you were screaming at me and trying to discour-

age me, I was looking in your eyes. In those eyes I saw a man in great pain. A man who's confused and afraid. Afraid of a tyrant father, who could very much destroy the two of us; although, I'm willing to take the risk.

I also see a man who's still very much in love with me. It's fine for now, I will make it…I always have. I'm a little more mature now and don't scar quite so easily. And I have my work…thank God for that. And you'll see one of my plays one day and there will be two actors playing us in a round-about way, but you'll know that those two actors are a testament to us.

Even though I don't have you, I still have memories, and they are beautiful…there aren't too many bad ones. The word I would use to describe my memories is "bliss." That's what life was like with you Larry. Blissful! All the way from the shaving cream to Veal Chanterelle at Café Des Artiste. I almost forgot making love. That's a tough one, not making love with you…how do you stand it…I hardly can. Sometimes I miss you so much I ache to the bone. God, just one more night…for you to hold me…let me know it's all going to be fine…just fine.

I have to close now, because if I don't, I'm going to cry. No, sob… that's what will happen. Thank you for bringing me back to life for a very long time. Larry I still love you and my instincts tell me you still love me too. If it's true don't wait too long. I like being with someone and I might settle for less waiting for you.

I Will Always Love You,
Drew

The Importance

The importance of all of this
Is that hopefully I have helped someone…
Someone who has loved
And cherished
And has had high hopes…
Only to see them dashed to bits
On the rocky shores of life
And is not sure they can ever try again
And not only that…doesn't give a rat's ass
If they ever love again…
Who are we kidding,
Of course, we want to love again.

Maybe it has helped…
Me putting all this down…
Maybe not…I'm not sure…

I hope you read this one day Larry,
I hope you know how I really feel deep down…
On a base level…
You're not at fault…
I'm not at fault…
We just did what humans do to each other…
We committed the unpardonable sin…
We loved,
And damnit, how we loved!
A bruised heart requires more time to heal

Than one that has suffered a major heart attack.
And when it heals, it stays tender...
But very guarded.
I need to thank you though
Thank you for prying open the lock...
Making the drawbridge fall down to
Cover the moat of loneliness
So that love could come marching in
Like a friggin' brass band I might add
On this prolific journey
Down the paper paths of this collection
Of my not so private any longer thoughts...
I have learned so much
And have experienced my self-pity and sorrow
Becoming a valuable lesson in my life.
Shit I can't say exactly what it's supposed to be,
But old Drew here is famous,
For doing things like filling up his canoe
With rocks when he's out rowing...
Or buying a picture frame...
It might be silver from Tiffany's
Or
A plastic frame from Woolworth's
Or
Art Deco from an auction at Phillip's
Or
A Gucci from Gucci.
The point is...
I have to learn that once I get the frame
I must stop trying to decide what the picture

Is going to be...
It's never the way I imagine it...
Ever... it's always different,
And sometimes the picture doesn't work in Art Deco!

I have my friends...(our friends)
Let's share them on alternate weeks,
And this incredible city
And my memories of a beautiful three years of my life
With you...
And a heart that knows how to love!

And that's about all I have to say
About being loved...
For now...except...

...There's nothing sadder
Than the grayness of Manhattan
on a snowy day
As you see it
From the floor-to-ceiling window
of your oh-so-drop-dead
Decorated-to-death Upper Westside apartment
With the view of
Central Park
And you have nothing to do,
And you are alone,
And it's a snowy day,
And the fireplace is roaring

And you don't want to be alone
On this snowy day...
On this snowy day.
But for now, I guess it's okay...

Epilogue

I thought about leaving you hanging,
Wondering what happened to Drew and Larry,
If you're a romantic you care…
If you're reading this in a doctor's office,
You're probably just killing time.
But for those of you who have the question,
And want it answered, here goes,
Remember now, this is Drew talking to you.

About eight months after Larry,
And a lot more pain and thinking,
I decided to settle…
I was sitting in a casting session for a new play I'd written,
When an actor in his early thirties stormed the stage,
And grabbed us by the short hairs with his audition.
He was a hunk, and gorgeous with Caribbean blue eyes
Jet black hair and a body that rippled
Like wheat waving in the August sun.
He wasn't reading the part, he was the part!
His name was Scott McVay,
Black Irish and Spanish…
The room went up ten degrees when he walked in.
Of course, I tried not to stare,
But he mesmerized me.
I told the director and the casting director
That he was who I had in mind
When I wrote that part.

Even though I had never met him,
He got the part.
It never occurred to me that there was a chance for romance,
And besides it's dangerous to mix work with pleasure.

A week later I went to a dinner party
At a friend's co-op on Riverside Drive overlooking the Hudson.
As I was looking at place cards,
Just in case I had to change mine,
And I would if I knew in advance
My dinner partner was boring.
The name next to mine was Scott McVay.
I chuckled at the irony, and looked forward
To chatting with my dinner partner.
He was perfectly charming and intelligent as well,
Also, gay and manly as they come.
No one would suspect him of being gay
As there wasn't a feminine or nelly bone in his body.

I know you're wondering…
How did he compare to Larry?
Not the same…
Handsome is handsome,
And chemistry is chemistry,
I wasn't sure at first,
But as dinner progressed
I thought I felt his knee brush mine
It did, and he left it there,
And I was getting horny as Hell.

Screw the rules,
I wanted to see this young man just for a lark.

I left a few minutes before him just to think,
And stopped at the Works
To have a nightcap.
It hadn't been fifteen minutes when Scott walked in.
We talked some more
And before I knew it,
It was two in the morning,
So I invited him back to the apartment
For coffee that never got made.
Without going into detail
He was fabulous in bed that night,
And the next morning,
And the next afternoon,
And that night and the next morning.
I insisted he move in which he did.
For a year we had a torrid love affair;
He liked my brain, I liked his everything.

I have to hand it to Scott…he had a lot of balls.
He was upfront and told me
He loved me,
But was not in love with me,
But was comfortable with me.
He also had experienced
The great love of his life…
And was still in mourning for that love.
He asked me

If I would beef up his part in the play
And make it a star-making role,
Because he wanted to go to Hollywood
To become a movie star.
I said yes…I would help him
He told me I was hot in the sack.

The play got raves…
Scott got raves…
And an offer to go to Hollywood
To test for a film which he got.
He wanted me to go with him
And write him a great film.
I said I would write the film,
But I was not going back to Hollywood
I'd be afraid to come home again
And relive Larry and me.
He was really sad I wasn't going,
But he understood.
Scott couldn't have known,
But I never shared all my emotions with him…
No, I learned that lesson very well.
However, he also didn't know
That I had fallen in love with him.
But with some time on my heart after Larry,
I weighed all the options.
I had a feeling that once he got to Hollywood
He would turn many heads…
No, New York is a safer shelter for my heart.

Sadly the day came for him to leave,
And I went down stairs with him.
As we came out of the building
One of the doormen came roaring up
In a shiny new black SAAB convertible.
My gift to Scott for keeping me warm during the winter
And letting me feel loved again...
It was really tough,
Going upstairs to that apartment.
But I did it...
Well, the first thing I looked at
Was a picture of Billy Rutger,
And damn it to Hell the tears came,
As they haven't since Larry and I broke up.
I felt so empty and dead...
But thanked God for my health,
My talent, my career,
And the drop-dead view.
Then I decided to watch some movies,
Make a bowl of popcorn, and be a kid again.

Two weeks later,
The headline in the paper screamed...
"LAWRENCE BARTON, WEALTHY INVESTMENT, BANKER SHOT TO DEATH!"
You cannot imagine the scream that escaped my lips.
As I read on,
I found it was Larry's father, not him.
It seemed that Ruth Lawrence,
The woman whose career he had ruined,

Had become an alcoholic.
And eventually became institutionalized for several years.
Once she sobered up,
She realized she wasn't nuts
And spent years trying to be released as
Old Barton was trying to keep her there.

Someway or the other
She got a note to a reporter who did one of those
"Whatever Happened To" columns
Which led to Ruth's case being heard,
Resulting in her release,
Along with a huge settlement from New York State
For being held all those years without justification.
As crazy as they thought she was,
She kept a journal, recording
Every moment she was there.
The one thought that kept her going
Was that when she got out,
She was going to kill Lawrence Barton
For ruining her career and life,
And that's precisely what she did!
I sent condolences to the family,
And purposely did not contact Larry,
Other than to send him a sympathy card.
He had seemed so final when we last spoke,
That I just assumed he still wanted to live his life
Away from me.
About two weeks after his father's death
There was a knock at my front door.

I opened it thinking it was the handy man
Coming to fix a leaky faucet.

The first thing I saw when I opened the door,
Were the most gorgeous green eyes
I have ever been lost in.
A gasp escaped my lips…
Larry was standing there,
With tears running down his cheeks…
And in a hoarse whisper, asked if he could come in.
I was in such a daze,
I just motioned him into the living room.
He was sheepish and shy like a naughty little boy.
He put his fingers to my lips,
And asked me not to say anything,
But to let him talk.

He said, "Drew you probably hate me…
And I can't blame you.
I have hurt you so deeply and painfully,
That you can never forgive me…
And I don't blame you if you can't,
Or when I finish if you ask me to leave…
Thank you for the card.
I didn't love him, but he was my father.
I've been so miserable trying to live
A life for him instead of me.
I feel as if I almost destroyed you,
And I deserve no forgiveness for that.
I came to beg if you want me to.

If there's just the smallest shred
That you still love or care about me,
I'd like to be in your life again.
I've never stopped loving you…
You made my life complete, whole, and worthy.
Just think about what I'm asking.
Please, let me back in your life.
I will give up the stock market…
Hell, I'll take a job in housewares,
At Bloomies if that's what it takes.
Anything!
God, I love you so much,
And miss the life I had with you.
All I'm asking is that you think about it.
Take all the time you need.
Can we love again…please?"

Can we love again? he asked.
To which I replied,
"I'm sort of set in my ways now…
I've learned to do things on my own,
Without having to answer to anyone.
I don't have to be responsible to anyone except myself…
I guess I can forgive you for almost destroying me,
And what I mean by that is,
I never loved so hard or beautifully.
You pried open my soul wider than the Hudson.
Your love presented me with feelings
And essences for life and the world…

A world I never knew existed.
And then you left so cowardly, and you did!
It's as if the darkest storm moved into my soul,
Slowly dousing the fires you had set within me.
It was a coldness that was unimaginable,
As was the pain that commandeered my life.
Slowly I healed and through that healing,
I wrapped another layer…
Around my heart for protection."
I slowly looked up at him and said,
"Can we love again?
No, we can't and here's why.
Because every time I leave the apartment,
Just for an errand or to meet a friend for lunch,
I would always wonder if you would be there,
When I returned."

To which Larry replied,
"I would always be there."
He could see by the look on my face…
That I had made my decision.
He asked, "Could I just hold you one more time,
Like I did when you were mine?"
I shook my head no…Goddamn that was hard.
I stood there frozen as he turned to go.
I heard the door click,
And held it together long enough
To pour myself a Cognac,
Then sat in front of the fire and let it go,

Until I was sure there were no more tears
For that man, not one more fucking tear!

I threw myself into my work and wrote,
A new play and called it *The Story of Us*.
My agent sent it out as soon as the ink was dry,
And before you knew it,
There were three offers to produce.
One day the phone rings,
And I knew the voice when he said hello.
It was Scott.

He told me he missed me,
And that he realized he loved me.
He said he had some time off before
His next film started and,
He wanted to come home and visit me.
I think it was the way he said "home."
And I said, "Yes, come on home."
He didn't quite make it home.
You know how actors are.
His agent called the day before
He was to leave for New York
With an offer for a star-making role.
He called, he asked, and I said, "Take it!"

Well shit,
Another Goddamn snowy Christmas.
I had made a lot of plans for us this Christmas,
Including a day-after flight to Playa del Carmen.

Oh well, the best laid plans.
So, here I am again.
Drop dead view from the windows.
Looks like another play is bubbling up
In this old head of mine.
Let me just get through Christmas and Hanukkah.
If you haven't guessed, I decided to embrace my religion again.
I'm really enjoying it.
I can't believe how many mothers
Are throwing their sons at me.
That's a switch.

It's two years later and,
Scott is a huge film star,
Who is being very coy about his sexuality.
The paparazzi are always on his ass,
So, he has to be very careful.
We meet occasionally at my beach house in Quogue.
It's more of a friendship with benefits.
I'm not complaining and maybe that's the way it will be.
I've had the love of my life, and doubt,
If I will find another one like that.

After meeting with my agent,
I packed a few things,
And threw them in my jade green Jaguar,
Then took off for Quogue.
There's something about the ocean,
A roaring fire, books, videos, and,
A bottle of Remy-Martin Cognac.

Well happy fucking holidays I said to myself.
No sooner did I arrive than the phone was ringing.
It was my neighbor calling to invite me
For Christmas Dinner.
He was having a few friends in from the city.
I agreed to come.

My neighbor Murry,
A new play producer,
Has a quirky shingle-covered house
That could have been right out of a Hallmark card.
A Menorah and a Christmas tree
Wreath on the door.
All bases covered.
I arrive on time and was handed
A Scotch and soda.
Murry said we were waiting for one more guest
Who was driving up from the city.
It's crazy, but the snow began to fall
As I watched the flames dance in the fireplace.
My mind began to drift back to another happier time,
But I heard myself say, "no, we're not going there."
The roasting turkey filled the air,
And I felt a smile cross my face.
The last guest arrived and I turned to meet
The most handsome face with the greenest eyes.
I couldn't believe it
Larry was standing there looking
As stunning as the first time I met him.

I stood there transfixed trying to figure out how
I could gracefully get the Hell out of there.

Before Larry could say anything,
I went to the kitchen where I told our host,
That I wasn't feeling well and was going home.
I don't know what would have happened had I stayed.
Would I have gotten drunk and maybe ruined the holiday?
I didn't want to find out.
As soon as I got in the door,
I threw some more wood on the fire,
Turned on the television for noise,
Fixed a drink and sat by the fire
With a throw on my lap.
Of course, then all the memories came flooding back.
The movie that came on that night,
Was *The Way We Were*,
Which I promptly shut off.
I decided to read a new book.

I guess I dozed off.
There was a knocking at the door.
I got up to open it,
And of course, it was Larry.
I tried to shut the door,
But he put his foot in to keep the door from closing.
"We're going to talk," he said.
Resigned, I let him in and motioned
For him to sit.
"Okay, let her rip," I said.

"I get it, you're still angry.
You have a right to be. I hurt you deeply.
I have searched my soul and,
If I could change anything I did, I would.
I've left you alone because I heard about
Your affair with Scott.
But when I saw you tonight,
I thought I have to give it one more chance."
He sat down and looked around, then at me.
"Well," I thought to myself, "is he crazy?"
Then all the good times came flooding back
And a MAYBE popped up in my head.
"Are you saying you still love me?" I asked.
"I never stopped, and if there is anyway
You'd give me a trial run,
 I would be forever grateful," he said.

Let me just say this.
Thank God, I had enough sense to say yes.
We've been together for five years now.
I don't wonder if he's going to be there when I come home.
He's there and so am I on this snowy day.
On this snowy day!

Dedicated

To

GorDON REYnolds

You were my first

Acknowledgments

I would like to thank Ben Harper and Ben Franczuski for posing for the cover. Jack Lowrance and Richard Gaz for the location. Paulo Murillo for the beautiful photography. Chris Capcia for my headshot photo. Patti Cappalli Taylor for the first read through. Janis Dworkis for her guidance in getting this book from there to here. P.W. for breaking my heart and giving me the reason to write this book. My beautiful and talented friend Peggy Lauren Lohr for her sustaining support and friendship. Robert Kilgore who captains my ship, and my Higher Power who directs my thinking and guides me.